Dicing with the Gods

Grug Smash Book 1

Sean McKenzie

Cover art by KittyPixels.

ISBN: 978-0-9950887-0-2

DEDICATION

For Sam and Henry, because it's never too late to fulfill a dream.

CONTENTS

ACKNOWLEDGMENTS

Thanks to Warren Marusiak and Robyn Wideman, who helped push me into writing again.

Very special thanks to Jeff St. Onge, who patiently picked through a very rough first draft and provided some polish.

CHAPTER 1

AUSPICIOUS BEGINNINGS

Grug barely heard the trap click beneath him before he plunged through the floor and into the water below. Fragments of what had seemed to be a perfectly sound floor tile slid past, as Grug's brain belatedly called "it's a trap!" The current was strong, and Grug could hear the shouts of his companions growing fainter each time his head thrust out of the water. Already, he could feel himself tiring from fighting his way to the surface. Taking a deep breath, he plunged under again and began twisting and thrashing his way out of his mail hauberk, cursing as the weight dragged him down to skip off the bottom of the waterway.

Finally free of his mail, Grug swam back to the surface and let his body relax into the current, trying to figure out where he was. In the dim light, filtering through cracks in the floors above, the water stretched as far as Grug could see, dotted with waist-thick pillars of rough, grey granite that kept the building from crashing down on top of him. Only faint lights coming through cracks from the floor above, and the soft glow of a peculiar moss that wound its way up the pillars saved the seemingly endless room from pitch darkness.

Grug grabbed onto one of the pillars as the current drew him past. For a moment he hung on, the massive muscles of his arms and shoulders bunching and twisting as he fought for a handhold on the moss-covered stone, before the water ripped him away, pulling him farther downstream. Brows furrowed, Grug continued to float, his mind grinding slowly through other ways he could free himself from the current's pull. At last, he tried again, steering his body in front of one of the pillars, and latching onto it with both arms and legs. For a moment, the water pinned the mighty barbarian, crushing him into the rock. Grug groaned as his crotch ground painfully into the pillar, and the pressure forced the air from his lungs. Finally, he reached up one long, muscled arm to find a handhold above the slimy moss, and slowly dragged his body from the sucking, unstoppable waters.

Grug peered into the gloom, his eyes searching for anything that might offer him a way out of the watery tomb. Finally, his eyes lit upon an irregular square outline of light in the ceiling above—a smuggler's hole to move cargo from the level above, downstream and out of the temple. Grug frowned fiercely at the waters rushing by below him, wondering how he could possibly traverse the distance from his pillar over to where the square of light beckoned.

Reaching up to the heavy beams that stretched between pillars, Grug searched for, and found, the heavy iron bolts holding the hewed timbers together. Slowly, carefully, Grug eased himself over the rushing waters, the bones in his hands and forearms creaking as he held to the bolts by only his fingertips.

"Grug getting too old for this," Grug thought sourly as he passed the halfway mark, his tongue poking from the corner of his mouth and his body swinging gently as he carefully shifted from bolt to bolt, the gritty rust beneath his fingertips threatening his grip with each movement.

Arriving finally at the pillar nearest the smuggler's hole, Grug gripped it between his thighs and stretched his upper body out toward the faintly lit outline. Gently, Grug worked his knife around the edges of the trapdoor, searching for the latch. It gave way with a sharp click, sending the hinged square of floor squealing downward, narrowly missing Grug's face. Grug cursed himself for not thinking to look for the hinges before working the latch, then grabbed hold of the hole's edge and pulled himself into the chamber above.

*   *   *

The room was nearly five paces square and almost as dark as it had been beneath its floor. Had it not been for a head-sized hole high in the wall, and the torchlight shining through, just right, onto the floor, Grug might never have seen the smuggler's hole from below. Short tables, covered in dusty objects, lined the walls of the small, square room, but for a massive, iron-strapped door. Grug smiled at the glint of gold amongst the objects, his eyes tracing through the bounty before landing on an old armour rack in one corner. The rack loomed like a forgotten scarecrow, a silver circlet tilting drunkenly where a helm should sit, and a strange, heavy pendant hanging from the slight, wooden neck. Grug drew closer, his eyes riveted on the pendant, though he could not say why; the chain looked to be nothing but forged iron links, something a maester would wear, with a simple obsidian cube in place of a jewel, but Grug could almost hear it speaking to him, calling for him to pick it up. The meager shards of reflected torchlight seemed to slide like oil across the surface of the stone, and Grug found himself drawn into the gentle play of colours and lights.

Faint shouts from outside the room pulled Grug's eyes to the reinforced oaken door. Recognizing the voices of his party, Grug put his mighty shoulders beneath the bar and strained to lift it. His body shook, the muscles of his legs twisting and shuddering, but the damp air swirling up through the smuggler's hole had rusted everything solid and immovable, even for his barbarian strength; despite his straining, the metal didn't even groan. Looking closer, Grug could see that rust caked the bar like dried blood, and corrosion bonded the metal to the bands of the door and frame.

Reaching over his shoulder, Grug grabbed for his war axe, staring with some amazement at his hand when it came back empty. Apparently, he had shrugged off more than his chain mail in the waterway. Taking quick stock of the situation, Grug struggled to see how the padded leather doublet, rough canvas pants, or thick leather boots he'd worn could be of much use in opening a rusted door.

"Grug in here!" he yelled in frustration, his massive fist slamming against the door. "Help Grug!"

The sound of heavy footsteps and clinking armour grew louder, as Grug continued to thump on the door. Finally, an answering tap came from the other side.

"Lad, is tha' you?" Grug felt relief wash over him at the sound of Bhalon's voice. The cleric had always been kind to Grug, looking after him like an older brother, and standing up for him against the other members of their party.

"It Grug. Grug stuck."

"If stuck is all ye' are, you're a sight better than we expected, seein' ya go through tha' floor," Bhalon replied. "We though' you migh' ha' drowned. Always were a lucky bastard, though."

Grug grunted.

"Is the door barred, Lad? Can ye' lift it?"

"Bar stuck. Need help."

"All right, Lad. I'll get Haeronor. Mayhap he'll have a spell that 'ill do the job."

The heavy footsteps receded down the corridor and Grug turned back to the room. Peering along the tables, and beneath them, Grug searched for anything he might use as a level to pry at the bar, though he was quickly distracted by the room's riches. Amongst old statues, jewels, and weapons were forgotten riches that would pay for Grug's lodging and food for more than a year, but ultimately it was the heavy pendant that drew his eye again. Walking over to the armour stand, Grug carefully undid the clasp, his broad fingers surprisingly deft. The obsidian sat heavily in his palm, drinking in the light on its facets and glimmering at its edges. Testing one side with his thumb, Grug found that the edges had been left sharp: equal parts beauty and danger. The darkness of the stone seemed to expand as he gazed into it, light swirling in iridescent patterns that ensnared his eyes as they danced. Grug found himself staring at the stone, unsure of how long he had stood there, being drunk into the stone, as the light was.

Footsteps sounded outside the door again, and Grug could hear voices arguing. He walked back over to the door, putting his ear next to the door frame to better make out what was being said.

"He's hardly worth the scroll," Grug could hear once voice say. A meaty thump followed, and pained wheeze.

"He's one of our party, Haeronor," Bhalon hissed, "and he's saved your arse more times than I'd care to count. Who was it that dragged you out of that rock troll's cave, not a month back."

"He's a liability!" Haeronor hissed back. "We're better off without him—or have you forgotten about how he set off the trap in the vampire's lair the month before that, and nearly got us all killed?"

There was a very pregnant pause. Grug could imagine the cold, unfriendly look on Haeronor's elven face even with the door between them. Then Bhalon's gravelly voice rumbled like a hive of angry bees: "You'll do it, or I'll crack yer skull and let the High Lord's light in myself. Maybe that will give you some sense."

"Fine." Soft footsteps traced back up the corridor. "Stand back."

There was a shuffling away from the door. "Grug," Bhalon called, "ye'd best step back from the..."

A howling shriek eclipsed Bhalon's words. Grug was thrown to the floor as a massive fireball crashed into the door, vaporizing the wood and sending metal shards spinning through the room. Grug's head pounded and he struggled to focus his eyes on the vague shapes coming through the door, framed by the torchlight now streaming in smoking hole where the door once sat.

Bhalon came straight to Grug's side, the dwarf's long red hair and beard bristling over immaculately-polished armour and deep blue surcoat. “All righ' there, lad?” Bhalon asked, his voice distant and muffled in Grug's ears.

Grug nodded, his vision still swimming. Irritably, he picked a small piece of hot metal out of the flesh of his forearm and dropped it to the floor.

Bhalon reached down, helping Grug to his feet and bracing the barbarian. Grug leaned gratefully on the dwarf as he regained his equilibrium.

“You're welcome, by the way,” Haeronor muttered, irritably brushing dust off of his long, purple and black wizard's robes. Cleaning complete, the willowy, elven mage turned his attention to the tables. “Hmm...spell scrolls, some nice gold work here, too. Maybe you're not completely useless after all, Grug.” He flashed a false smile, his steely-blue eyes full of contempt.

“I wouldn't go that far,” Triwathon drawled. The tall, graceful elven ranger sidled in the door, his bow strung and an arrow resting on the string. “We might be better off with a trained monkey. At least it would be cheaper to feed.”

Rage clouded Grug's vision and tripped up his tongue, as it always seemed to. Only Bhalon's steadying hand and his own splitting headache kept him from driving a fist into Triwathon's face.

Haeronor chuckled. “Now, now, Triwathon. Don't make our

barbarian friend too angry. Remember what happened to that thief that tried to cut his purse last week."

Grug grimaced. Honestly, he hadn't meant to pull the fellow's arm off. It was an accident. He was only trying to make him drop the purse he had cut from Grug's belt.

The reminder seemed to be enough for Triwathon, who moved past Grug and began his own tally of the treasures on the tables.

"Not bad," Haeronor said finally, as he finished examining the last table and turned his eyes to the circlet still sitting on the armour stand. "Even if this is all we find in the temple, the trip has been more than worth it. I'll take the scrolls, of course; no one else can cast them. The rest we can split four ways."

Grug's brows lowered. Even he knew that the scrolls were worth more than the rest of the treasure combined. "No cheat Grug."

The mage turned. "Cheat Grug? That fireball spell I just used to open the door was worth more than you are, human. You're lucky to get anything at all." He spied the necklace still clutched, forgotten, in Grug's fist. "That should go into the common pile, as well."

Grug looked down at the pendant. It was ugly, likely worthless to all but a blacksmith, who might melt the chain down and make something useful. Certainly not something to argue over. "No. This Grug's."

The mage's eyebrow arched and all traces of humour vanished from his face. "Put it in the pile, Grug, or I will make you wish you had."

An animal growl vibrated in Grug's chest. In two quick steps, he was across the room, and Haeronor swung a foot off of the floor, the collar of his robes lost in Grug's massive fist. Grug pulled the mage close. "This Grug's."

Elven eyes were suddenly awash in golden flames and an

incantation began to roll off of Haeronor's tongue in a musical elven language that sounded simultaneously enticing and foreboding. Steel sung on leather from behind Grug as Triwathon unsheathed his slim dagger and started toward the pair.

"Enough, Haeronor!" Bhalon snapped, "Unless you want t' find out how yer spells stand up to the High Lord's power." His eyes swung to Triwathon. "Or how tha' knittin' needle fairs against my mace."

Haeronor's incantation trailed off and his eyes slowly bled back to blue, though they still glittered with suppressed fury. Triwathon glared at the stocky cleric, but slipped his dagger back into its belt sheath.

"Ye know those scrolls are worth more than the rest," Bhalon continued, his gaze back on the mage. "You'll take them as yer quarter, and you'll bloody well be ready ta use them if *any* member of this party needs you to." Haeronor nodded reluctantly. "And let the boy keep 'is prize; it looks to be worth little enough as i' tis. Grug, put him down."

Grug opened his fist. Only Haeronor's elven grace saved him from sprawling on the floor. Grug took a step back and, with exaggerated slowness, fastened the pendant around his thick neck, his eyes never leaving the mage's.

Hate shone in Haeronor's eyes.

"Let's divide this up and get movin'." Bhalon said. "We've still got a maiden to save—and a guardian to slay, no doubt."

CHAPTER 2

AWAKENING

The walls of the temple corridor were rough stone, damp from the waters below and lit with a combination of flickering torches and strange, round lights that connected to narrow pipes stemming from the walls. Grug found himself wondering who tended the torches, all of which seemed to be new and nearly smokeless. Surely, some of them should have burned down by now. More importantly, if the corridor was important enough to warrant being lit, then where were all of the people?

The party's footsteps echoed off the walls around them, loud enough to warn any guards of their coming, but the temple remained empty, and eerily silent. Grug shifted his hands nervously on the haft of his new war axe, found under a table in the smuggler's room. The air's dampness had rusted the double-bladed iron head, but a few strokes with Grug's sharpening stone had revealed sound beveled edges, and a few more left the edges bright and deadly sharp. Unconsciously, Grug tested the edge with his thumb—sharp, but not so sharp as to unnecessarily risk nicking the blade.

As they passed a set of torches set closer together than most of the ones they had seen in the corridors, something tickled at Grug's awareness. He couldn't quite put his finger on what it was, but there was something odd about the torches, and the wall between them. He slowed for a closer look, and tried to focus, but his mind wandered. He glanced over at one of the round lights and wondered suddenly if the pipe it connected to was hollow, and if it provided some sort of fuel. Grug had never seen a light of that kind, but he could vaguely remember being told about an alchemist that could do something like that, once. He hadn't really understood at the time; he had heard something said about 'gas,' chuckled to himself, and wandered off to look at some of the curiosities in the old man's shop.

Abruptly, Grug realized that the rest of the party had wandered out of sight. Not keen to listen to another tirade from Haeronor about his stupidity, Grug broke into a jog. With uncharacteristic doggedness, Grug's mind wandered back to the lights and their tubes. He felt like he had almost worked out an answer when he turned a corner and knocked Triwathon sprawling. Haeronor turned, one hand enveloped in flame and ready to fight; Bhalon just turned and shook his head.

“Sorry,” Grug muttered to Triwathon, extending a hand to help the elf to his feet. “I didn't mean to do that.”

Triwathon clearly wasn't in a mood to listen. He sprang to his feet with a look of indignation and stalked after Haeronor and Bhalon like an angry cat.

Grug turned to follow, but a glint of light caught his eye. Caught in a crack between the floor stones and the wall was a piece of mirror. He squatted down on his haunches to get a closer look, and pulled it carefully from the crack. It was at least a full finger long, and as thick as Grug's pinkie—clearly it had been broken from a larger piece and lost down in the corridor, but a quick look around showed Grug no evidence of more pieces, as one might see if a mirror was dropped, nor had he seen any decorations on the walls; they were plain stone, all, except for the torches and lights. Again, Grug felt a light tickle in his mind, a light touch that he could almost believe he had imagined. He wanted to probe at it, needed to, like a child sticking their tongue into the socket of a lost tooth, but already Haeronor and the rest of the party were nearing another corner, and he dared not lose sight of them again.

Grug caught up to the other three just as Haeronor came to a stop—once again in front of the two oddly spaced torches.

"Damnation," Haeronor spat. "This is the third time we've passed this same place, I'm sure of it!"

Bhalon scratched his bearded cheek irritably. "Aye. I thought mayhap i' was just a like corridor the second time, but this is ridiculous. Those ha' got to be the same torches, and tha's the same scrape down the wall, there. We're goin' in circles."

"Impossible," the mage argued. "I thought the same when we passed here a second time; I took completely different turns. How could we end up back here again?"

Grug turned away as Haeronor and Bhalon continued their argument, watching back the way they had come to make sure no one could sneak up on them. He gazed back at the torches, which did not seem to have burned down in the time they had been wandering through the temple halls. As Grug's eyes followed the flickering lights and the answering reflections from the edge of his axe, a clattering sound, like bones clicking together, filled his head. He spun back to the others, axe at the ready, but Haeronor and Bhalon continued their argument, while Triwathon cleaned his fingernails idly with a dagger tip. Clearly, none of the others could hear the sound.

The rattling was gone as abruptly as it had come, and Grug found himself staring at the wall opposite the two torches—though he couldn't quite have said why. He stepped closer, eyes wandering over the plain grey stone, and felt his gaze drawn to one small fissure in particular, which he was nearly certain was the precise size and shape of the mirror shard he had picked up. Slowly, he placed the piece of mirror into the hole, pressing gently and waiting for the inevitable hidden door to open.

He was sadly disappointed.

Grug pushed the piece again, wiggling it as much as the hole would allow, but nothing happened. He took a few steps down the corridor and checked to make sure a door hadn't slid open silently without him noticing; again, nothing. Nonplussed, he turned back up the corridor and started back to join Bhalon and the others, but stopped when he realized that the little shard was reflecting light from the torches onto the wall. While this wasn't exactly a stunning turn of events, Grug was astounded to see that what he had taken to be merely more cracks and fissures in the wall were in fact some sort of writing, visible only in the reflected light.

"Bhalon."

The dwarf turned, his finger still pointing angrily at Haeronor's chest. "Not now, Grug. We're trying to decide which way we should go." He turned back to the elf.

"Bhalon," Grug repeated, "bring me your shield."

The stocky cleric sighed, unstrapped his burnished silver shield and brought it over to Grug. "Now what's all this about?"

Taking the shield, Grug turned back to the torch, turning until the reflected light fell where he had seen the letters appear. The surface of the wall rippled like a curtain in the wind, and the entire message appeared, letters hewn into the stone itself. Grug lowered the shield, but the words remained.

Bhalon looked at Grug in open astonishment as he took his shield back from the barbarian. "Well done, Lad. Well done, indeed."

Soft steps hurried down the corridor. "By Anor!" Haeronor whispered, looking at Grug in amazement. "This is a primordial script. How did you...?"

Grug shrugged. "I don't know. It just...felt like the right thing to do.

What does it say?"

"I..." Haeronor turned back to the message, his eyes still wide and a little wild. "I don't know. Perhaps I could try cross-referencing it with draconic, or something of that sort." He began digging through his bag of holding, various scrolls appearing and disappearing as he searched for one in draconic. He maintained a constant commentary, almost babbling, as though he had just seen a ghost he knew, or a dragon he didn't.

Grug ignored the mage, turning back to the message and gently running his fingers across the letters. Loops joined with gentle curves and sharp strike-throughs in beautiful intricate patterns, baffling, and yet...There were clearly repetitions, to Grug's eye: patterns. A long hooked line repeated here, a crossed arc emphasized there—like a morsel of meat held just out of his reach.

Bones rattling like a dragon's skeleton falling down a hillside sent Grug jumping back from the wall and brandishing his axe once more. Bhalon had his mace out no more than a breath later, and Triwathon held his bow ready, an arrow already fitted to the string.

"What is it Grug?" Bhalon asked, spinning around to check both sides of the corridor.

The bones rattled on in Grug's ears. "Don't you hear it? Bones clicking together?"

Bhalon stood still a moment, listening, before slowly shaking his head. "No, Lad. I hear nothing but us and the torches." He looked to Triwathon, who shrugged; he had heard nothing, either. "Maybe they're rocks tumbling...but I didn't even see you shake your head to get them rolling around," the ranger drawled.

Grug ignored the insult; the bones had ended their clatter with a soft thump that seemed to come from the message itself, and Grug turned to stare at the letters once more. Pieces fell into place in Grug's mind and the hair on the back of his neck rose as the pattern seemed to shine with its own inner light, standing out from the stone and calling Grug's attention.

"Haeronor," Grug said, "look." The mage frowned irritably, but watched as Grug's fingers, thick as sausages, trailed gently over the letters. "These same few words are repeated over and over, if you ignore some of the swirls over top of them. I think...I think they're directions."

Haeronor stared at Grug openly, his mouth agape. Grug could feel Bhalon and Triwathon's eyes on his back and knew instinctively that they were likewise astounded. "How...?" Haeronor glanced at the words and nodded. "You're right, I think. But how did *you* know that?"

Grug shook his head slowly. "I don't know. It just seemed...right."

Bhalon stepped up beside Grug, his neck craned back to look up into the close-set brown eyes hiding beneath the barbarian's heavy brow. "Are ye all right, Lad? I've never heard ye call yerself anythin' bu' 'Grug,' much less see aught in another language, other than pretty pictures. And if'n I'm nah sorely mistaken, you may have spoken more words in these last few minutes than in the week before tha'."

Haeronor's eyes narrowed. "He's right. You're different. Why?"

Grug shrugged. "I don't know."

"That pendant!" Haeronor hissed, his gaze darting down to the obsidian stone hanging on Grug's chest. "I knew it must be more than it seemed. Give it to me!"

Grug stepped back, bumping into Triwathon and nearly knocking the ranger to the floor. "No! It's mine."

"Don't be a fool!" Haeronor railed. "It's clearly magical. It could be cursed! It could be demonic!" He advanced on Grug, golden light blooming around his hand and in his eyes.

Grug stepped back further, his back thudding solidly into the wall, and his axe already raised above his shoulders. "Get away from me, Haeronor! The pendant belongs to me!"

"Fool human!" Haeronor cried. "Even if the stone isn't cursed, surely it could be better used by someone already possessing a superior intellect." He stepped forward, hand reaching for the pendant.

Blinding silver light filled the corridor, sending Grug, Haeronor, and Triwathon to their knees, hands racing to cover their eyes. "Such as a mage?" Bhalon asked dryly, his holy light dimming and finally disappearing. "I do no' think so. The High Lord has seen fit ta bestow the pendant on Grug. So shall i' stay."

Haeronor came to his feet, fury etched in every line of his body. "Or a demon has. Do you think this fool would know the difference?"

"No," Bhalon smiled. "but I certainly would." He stepped over to where Grug still kneeled, reached up and gently took the obsidian stone in his hand. A soft, silver light suffused Bhalon. His eyes closed and his head tilted back toward the heavens. Grug felt a vague sense of amusement and a gentle brush, like a parent's hand ruffling his hair.

Bhalon's light winked out, leaving the corridor in the flickering shadows of the torches once more. "The High Lord approves," Bhalon intoned. "So shall it be." With a smile, the dwarf took Grug's arm and helped him to his feet. "Now, Lad. What else can you make o' tha' message?"

Grug stepped carefully past the still furious mage and leaned close to the wall. "This means right, I think. And this," he pointed to the next word, "is left. The last must mean to keep going straight. I think it's supposed to be the way forward to the temple."

Bhalon nodded. "Aye. Tha' seems likely, though I dunna know who migh' ha' left that sort of map for us to find. It may well be a trap."

"My thoughts exactly," Haeronor said haughtily.

"However," Bhalon continued, "I dunna see what other choice we have. I say we migh' as well try it."

Haeronor shared a glance with Triwathon, who shrugged gracefully, before turning back to Bhalon. "It's as good a plan as any. Let's hope the fool isn't leading us straight to our deaths." Without another word, Haeronor pulled a stylus from his pack and quickly copied the turns as Grug had described them. His leather boots squeaked softly beneath his robes as he spun and stalked up the corridor, leaving the rest of the party scrambling to keep up.

CHAPTER 3

OF MAIDENS AND STONE MEN

The chamber was enormous—far bigger than a temple under a mountain had any right to be, Grug thought—and it stretched into the shadowy distance beyond Grug's sight. Before them stretched a walkway nearly twenty fathoms long, cutting through what would more properly be called a lake than a rock pool. Tall, white columns stood on each side of the walkway, enticing visitors forward as though into a king's court, though Grug couldn't shake the feeling that he was more likely entering a slaughtering pen than a throne room. At the end of the walkway, a stairway rose toward a dais of polished marble with a throne in the centre. An enormous ebony idol, shaped like an ape, loomed over the throne's back; polished emerald eyes the size of hen's eggs seeming to follow the party as they made their way down jagged stone steps to the edge of the walkway.

The party advanced warily with Grug and Bhalon at the head, the fighters' massive shoulders forming an uneven wall in front of the archer and the mage. Grug stepped cautiously, remembering the floor tiles near the entrance, but the walkway felt sturdy enough to hold even his weight. In the pools to either side, Grug could make out dark shapes swimming, longer than he was tall. They darted this way and that, sleek and quick. Grug resolved to stay out the water.

When they had crept nearly half way along the causeway, Grug heard a grating sound from the dais and stopped, his eyes darting fearfully to the idol. Though the massive ape remained motionless, a dim light shone from behind the throne, where a door had opened in the wall of the mountain itself. The ostensibly solid rock yawned wide to reveal a slim, elven maiden in a long, linen dress.

Stepping past Grug and Bhalon, Haeronor marched forward a few steps, a confident smile on his face; clearly, this was the girl they had been paid to rescue and in some stroke of rare good fortune, it seemed they had not only found her, but found her unharmed and away from her captors. “Mae goveannen, brennil nin,” the mage intoned. “Glass nin gen govaded.”

Grug knew only a few words of elvish, enough to recognize the words as a greeting. His mind had just begun to pick apart the phrases further when a deep voice shook the chamber. “Fools!” the maiden boomed, in a voice clearly not her own. “Here you will find only death, and my children shall feed. Prepare yourselves!”

The elven maiden fell to the floor like a puppet with cut strings. Behind her, the idol's eyes blazed to life, shining with malevolence. Black rock swelled and surged as though alive, and an inhuman bellow sprang from the dark lips as the idol trudged forward toward the steps.

Grug heard crashes from both ends of the room, and looked up the way they had come. Two grey stone behemoths emerged, their granite skin grating and crashing as they stepped out of the very walls and moved to block the party's escape. A matching pair of behemoths stomped from the shadows at the far end of the room. Haeronor cursed as water splashed onto the walkway, and Grug saw, with some dismay, that the grey shapes had come to the surface: massive fish with dead eyes and enormous teeth that flashed crookedly from yawning mouths.

"Berio ven Eru," Triwathon whispered.

"Aye," Bhalon replied. "And may the High Lord watch over us, as well."

Stepping forth, the cleric slung his mace from his belt loop and held up his hand in supplication, his eyes closed and his lips moving silently in prayer. A silver hammer appeared in his fist, glowing as though afire with moonlight. "Come forth, daemon," Bhalon roared, his eyes springing open, "and meet yer end!"

Bhalon and Haeronor moved to meet the newly-animated idol, leaving the rest of the party to deal with the stone men. Triwathon began firing arrows at the two behemoths at the far end of the room, though they were unsurprisingly ineffective. Grug was already turning back to face the stone men racing down the stairs behind them, when a sound like gravel pouring over boulders rumbled through the room. Twisting and contorting their massive bodies, the granite men curled into themselves, rapidly reshaping into enormous stones. As Grug watched, the boulders rolled down the stairs, gaining speed with every second. If they managed to reach the walkway itself, the party would have no choice but to throw themselves into the water, or be crushed beneath the massive, rolling stones. After seeing the fish, Grug wasn't sure which option he feared more.

Dropping his axe, Grug dashed to the nearest column, hugging it to his chest and pulling back with all his strength toward the path. He cursed as his feet slipped at the water's edge, set himself again, and strained as though trying to uproot a tree. A groan escaped his lips as the column finally began to topple, its heavy lintel picking up speed as it crashed toward the ground. Grug threw himself to the side before he could be crushed, pushing against the column to throw himself closer to his companions.

With a mighty crash, the first spherical behemoth slammed into the column and spun away, landing in the water and sinking quickly out of a sight. Only the roll Grug had tucked into at the end of his jump saved him from being crushed by the pillar. The second behemoth struck the column a moment later, near the lintel. The collision sent it spinning into the air over Grug's head, toward the rest of the party.

"Bhalon!" Grug screamed.

The dwarf turned, eyes wide. Cocking his arm back, he heaved his hammer toward the rapidly approaching ball. The two met with an ear-splitting crack like a thunder-clap, and the behemoth flew back the way it had come. Grug had only a moment to register the skeletal clattering sound in his head before the edge of the sphere knocked him sprawling and his head crashed into the walkway. The dim light of the temple flashed to incandescence. Then there was only darkness.

* * *

Grug floated weightless in a void. Darkness slid like silk along his skin, winding around him, tunneling through his soul. Somewhere in the ether, three gods pleaded and argued with a fourth: "why would it have to be a twelve saving throw, Russell? It was just a glancing blow, even if he did miss the roll to dodge."

"Because it was a big friggin' rock, and he's lucky to be alive, let alone conscious. Now make the damn throw."

The voices grew faint, as Grug drifted onward through nothingness, but the sound of clattering bones grew louder, reverberating through his body like a second heartbeat.

The silk was torn from around him, the darkness now an ominous spectre instead of a comforting void. Soft light bloomed in his vision, and he felt a wrench, like a hook in his belly, pulling him upward toward the glow. As the darkness retreated, the pain in his body grew. Like a touchstone, it guided him back out of the void to be reborn in the light.

* * *

The rhythmic pinging of metal on stone pulled Grug back to the waking world. He opened his eyes slowly, his vision swimming, and tried to remember why he was in a cave. His body hurt, bruises and scrapes singing discordantly with the heavier aches of his chest and skull. Grug rolled slowly to his hands and knees, stomach roiling and breathed deeply, trying to order his thoughts.

Around him, the battle raged on. Bhalon darted deftly around the giant idol's legs, far faster than Grug would have ever expected of the stocky cleric, raining down blows with his heavy mace. Haeronor stood at a distance, casting magical bolts whenever his line of sight was clear, though his proud, haughty posture sagged with exhaustion. One of the two remaining stone men—Grug could only assume that the one that hit the lintel had also sunk into the water—looked to be little more than a pile of rubble, its legs and one arm shattered, and the other arm flopping ineffectively. Triwathon carefully evaded the final stone man's attacks, occasionally spinning closer to deliver blows with what looked to be a salvaged stone table leg—though where the ranger would have found it, Grug couldn't imagine. The ranger's slight body belied an impressive strength, and the stone man was slowly succumbing to his strikes, though stone chips rained off of his makeshift mace.

Grug pushed himself slowly to his feet, staggering a few steps and stooping to pick up his axe. He shambled down the walkway drunkenly, his equilibrium slowly returning, and watched as Bhalon spun his entire body into the swing of his mace, smashing it into the idol's knee. Unphased, the idol responded with an almost contemptuous slap, sending the dwarf flying back toward the stone steps, where he landed in a crumpled heap. The granite monstrosity turned its gaze to Haeronor, marching forward with grim purpose.

Grug broke into a run, adrenaline masking his hurt and fatigue. Realizing that it would do him little good in melee, Grug flung his axe at the idol's head, using the monster's momentary distraction to slip around it and scramble up its massive stone back. Drawing his dagger, Grug plunged it into the hollow between the idol's granite shoulder and its neck, praying that the stone there would be thinner. The blade broke with a metallic snap, spinning away down the monster's chest. With an angry roar, the idol shook itself like a wet dog and Grug could feel the wind whistling past him as he flew off the polished back and into the water.

Swearing, Grug fought to the surface and began swimming for the side of the pool as fast as he could, fear lending frantic strength to his arms and legs. Rattling bones echoed in Grug's head and he turned to see one of the monstrous fish arcing toward him, its smooth, muscular body propelling it through the waves like a javelin. Cold with terror, Grug pulled back his arm, hoping futilely to catch the fish on its snout and turn it away.

With a soft whistle, Triwathon's arrow sliced through the air above Grug's shoulder and buried itself in the fish's brain. Grug twisted out of the way as the grey body flopped and twitched, slamming one of its long fins into his midsection. Grug cursed, turned around, and swam swiftly to the edge of the rock pool, heaving himself out of the water before another of the fish decided to pursue him.

Grug nodded his thanks to Triwathon, who had downed the second stone man and was slowly limping his way to where Haeronor was desperately casting spells at the idol. Fire blazed from the mage's fingertips, icy cold poured from a scroll he clutched, but the granite daemon moved ever closer, malice steaming from his emerald eyes. With a roar, Grug leapt up onto the idol's back once more, feet scrambling momentarily on the smooth sides, before his muscled arm looped over one shoulder and gave him the purchase he needed to swing upward and straddle the back of the idol's neck.

With its eyes trained on the elven mage, the idol ignored Grug as though he were a fly, giving the barbarian the moment he needed to plunge his hand beneath the granite brow, grab hold of a glowing emerald, and pull with all his might.

The monster screamed in rage and pain as its eye pulled free in Grug's grasp. Its arms swung wildly, narrowly missing Grug's head, but the beast's shoulders were ill-suited to scratching its own back. Ducking and twisting his body to the other side, Grug grabbed hold of the second eye with his left hand, throwing himself backwards and letting the momentum of his fall tear the other eye from its socket.

Rolling as he hit the ground, Grug looked up to see the monster flailing wildly, casting about with its arms in the hopes of catching him.

"Triwathon!" Grug called, dropping the gems on the ground at his feet, and holding his hand out toward the ranger. Without a word, Triwathon tossed Grug what was left of his makeshift mace. Raising the table leg in both hands, Grug sent it crashing down onto one of the emeralds. The gem shattered, pieces flying in all directions, and the idol gave a rumbling scream that shook the cave and nearly deafened the party. The eyeless face turned toward Grug; the thick, granite legs churned as the monster threw itself toward the barbarian, but it was already too late. Grug raised the table leg over his head a second time and brought it down as though trying to drive it through the emerald before him and into the floor of the cave itself. The second stone flew to pieces, and the ebony idol fell to the floor with a force that knocked Grug to his knees. They had won.

Triwathon clapped Grug on the shoulder. "Well, you do know how to make an impression; I'll give you that." Grug wasn't sure who started laughing first, but the entire party was soon roaring with laughter—even Bhalon, who had come to and was reclined exhaustedly on the staircase behind him.

As the laughter trickled away, Bhalon pushed himself to his feet, swaying for a moment as he found his balance. "Well," he said, "I suppose we ha' best check on our maiden, hadn't we? Hopefully her singin' voice ha' recovered."

Haeronor led the way up the staircase, his face etched with exhaustion, but glowing in triumph. Kneeling next to the maiden, he spoke softly in elven, his gently glowing hand brushing her black hair back from her eyes. The maiden's eyes opened slowly, widening with fear as she took in their faces, no doubt wondering what fresh torments awaited her. Haeronor spoke quick, musical words in elven; Grug could pick out the words for father and rescue, but little else.

The maiden calmed, a tentative smile crossing her face. "Le hannon," she said softly. "Thank you."

CHAPTER 4

WHEN NOTHING IS NORMAL

Grug watched one of the barmaids bringing ale to a nearby table of labourers, his eyes tracing the lines of her body by habit for a moment before he realized where he was. Grug stared in shock at the warm, somewhat dingy common room that he always seemed to come back to. An open stone hearth stood in the center of the room, with circles of tables radiating out from it until they reached a row of booths on one side, the door to the street, the stairs to the rooms above, or the bar. The bar itself stood along one wall, staffed day and night (or so it seemed) by One-eyed Jack, a stout man with few hairs, an eye patch, and a cudgel that he kept beneath the bar for unruly customers. A second barmaid swept through the swinging door beside the bar, and the mouth-watering smells of fresh bread and roasting meat followed her out. Nothing about the room seemed out of the ordinary to Grug, but he had no idea how or when he might have arrived.

The trip back from the temple seemed to take no time at all, and Grug could scarcely remember the journey; no sooner had Bhalon said "let's return to town," then Grug was at a table in the One-Eyed Jack—his inn of choice— alone. That puzzled him, as well: why was it that he never seemed to see his party except when they were out on some sort of quest? He could vaguely remember times past when he would sit for weeks, waiting for Bhalon or Haeronor to show up with word of some demon that needed slaying or maiden that needed rescuing, but he saw nothing of them in the time between.

The barmaid smiled at Grug as she walked past his table. Though slight and pretty, she easily held five or six full tankards in each hand without any apparent effort, and her smile slipped only for a moment, when one of the men at the next table pinched her on the way past. Grug grinned into his tankard at the look in the barmaid's eyes. The man would be lucky if all he got in return was spit in his ale; he might just as likely have the next tankard split his skull.

Grug stopped mid-sip, the ale running down off of his chin and splashing coldly into his lap. When had he ever really known what was going on in someone's mind before, just from looking at their eyes? Hellfire, when had he ever really *wondered* about what was going on in someone's mind, outside of a fight? Grug fought a momentary urge to stop the barmaid and ask her exactly what she was thinking, and carefully placed his tankard back on the table.

Grug idly looked back at the man that had pinched the barmaid. With the deck of cards in the man's hand, it wasn't hard to guess what he was thinking, and the look on his face was one of pure wanting—be it money, or another grab at the barmaid. Grug had never been much of a card player himself. He could never tell if someone was bluffing.

A smile slowly crept across Grug's face. Maybe there was something to be said for knowing what was going on in other people's heads.

* * *

Grug stepped out of the inn a few hours later, into the late-afternoon sun. His purse was full near to bursting, despite a number of rounds bought for the entire bar. The man holding the deck of cards had been a very wealthy merchant, and the afternoon's dealings may have made a bit of a dent in that wealth. Grug wondered idly how long it would be before the man tried his luck at cards again.

A dry wind blew dust into Grug's mouth. It had been a dry summer in Shimano, almost unheard of in the coastal city, and the streets of the outer city swirled with dust. Only the horse manure kept the road from blowing away entirely. The inner city had fared somewhat better with its cobblestones, but even there the plants lay parched and dying. Grug preferred not to go there, anyway. The merchants were rude, the whores were expensive, and the inns served the same swill as the taverns in the outer city, but at twice the price.

Grug's amusement at his winnings faded with each step he took from the inn. As entertaining as it had been relieving the merchant of his money, it had been almost unnervingly easy. Without even trying, he had read the other man's face (he had the slightest quirk of an eyebrow when getting a good card, and tended to rub the ring finger of his left hand on the back of the cards when he was unsure, amongst other signs). After a few hands, Grug felt more like he was just waiting for the merchant to decide how much money to give him for each round. The longer they played, the more desperate the merchant became, and the easier it was to take what he had.

Grug felt guilty. Not *really* guilty—he couldn't help but feel that the merchant may have deserved a bit of poetic justice—but guilty enough. Without the amulet, he would have lost money faster than the merchant had.

Grug turned down the steep road leading to the harbour. Tension that he hadn't realized he was holding in his shoulders began to ease as he breathed in the tang of salt air. The water called to him, as it always did. He guessed that must be from his time as a sailor and pirate, on the... Grug stopped his tracks, smiling ruefully. It was silly that he had spent enough time on a ship to love the sea, but he couldn't remember the name of the ship. How many hours had he spent on the deck, the (two?)...(three?) masts towering above him, and the hemp undoubtedly scourging his hands until they grew tough as old boots.

Grug's smile turned into a frown as he tried, a little desperately, to remember the feel of the hemp in his hands, or the sway of the deck beneath his feet, but there was nothing. It was as though he recalled something he had seen in a painting—he could see the picture in his head, but not place himself in it.

Grug walked distractedly to a bench in front of a tailor's shop and sat down. He held his head in his hands as though hoping to prise his memories free, and cast about for anything that would serve as a lifeline—how to tie knots in rigging, what cargoes he had helped carry, even the names or faces of other sailors. Everything was blank, as though he had lived his life alongside half-carved children's dolls, faces still smooth and unfeatured, while he himself was nothing more than a passive observer—a child watching a play.

Grug dug farther back and tried to conjure his parents, his trek from the untamed highlands of Narran to the southern countries, meeting Bhalon and the rest of his party. There was nothing but blank faces and empty facts. Nothing from his past felt real.

Grug's mind raced. Bhalon. He had to find Bhalon. The cleric would know what to do. Grug surged to his feet, only to stare blankly at the road. Where could he find Bhalon? The dwarf was always at his side during a quest, guiding him and defending him, but Grug had no idea where Bhalon stayed when they weren't adventuring. He dug through his mind for any sense of where Haeronor or Triwathon might be—desperate enough to seek help even from the two of them—but he had only a vague idea that Haeronor lived in a mage's order of some kind, and that Triwathon preferred to camp outside of the city.

Grug's nostrils flared and his eyes rolled a panicked horse's. Struggling not to run, he made his way to the sea wall at the harbour's edge and leaned against it, chest heaving and lungs pulling in breath after breath of salty air. A beggar-child, his clothes nothing but filthy rags, came tentatively forward from the edge of the docks, proffering a wooden bowl, fear and desperation competing in his eyes as he watched the barbarian's brooding face and angry eyes. Grug forced a smile at the boy and tossed a copper into his bowl.

The beggar boy seemed to break the panicked cycle in Grug's brain, but it still worked furiously to find some sort of answer. Should he throw the pendant into the sea? Would that return his memories? Surely not. Like his sudden arrivals at the One-Eyed Jack, it seemed as though this was the way things had always been, even if he hadn't been able to see it without the amulet. Removing it might take his ability to reason, but he was icily certain that he would still remember what he had learned. Besides, Grug thought, wasn't it time that he had the respect he deserved from those who knew him? He was tired of being thought an idiot, and sick of being treated like one. Maybe he could even learn some beginner magic, just to spite Haeronor. Grug smiled ruefully at the thought of spinning spells, expecting a mage capable of summoning greater elementals to be impressed by some sparkling lights; maybe he would just stick with using his axe to impress people.

Grug watched the seabirds wheeling above him, screeching as they searched for food and fought amongst themselves. He wondered if soaring closer to the gods brought any more insight into why they did what they did. Why would they give him these powers? What did they want in return?

A bird plunged into the water. What if Haeronor had been right? What if it was a demon, not a god, that had done this? What if this was madness. All of the intelligence in the world couldn't tell him if the chord that thought struck within him was because he knew it to be true, or because he feared it was so.

Felling the fear rising in his chest and threatening panic once more, Grug took a deep breath and pushed away from the sea wall, walking slowly along the harbour and trying not to think of anything but the moment itself. The docks looked lonely and desolate, with cargos already unloaded for the day, but the markets that ran along the sea wall were still bubbling with people. The markets had always been a place of joy for Grug: the colorful and shiny wares from dozens of countries across the seas caught his eye; the strange and malformed fish from the deepest depths of the oceans sparked his interest; and the exotic women plying their trade inflamed his lust. Now, it seemed, all wonder had disappeared. Grug picked up a golden box and felt where the cheap paint had flaked away on the bottom. The greasy merchant selling it fawned, while his eyes appraised the amulet at Grug's throat and weighed his purse. Grug dropped the box back on the pile of garbage the merchant was trying to pass off as treasure, and walked on.

A prostitute, garbed in nothing but a short, blue linen skirt and a gauzy scarf, stood illuminated by the red rays of the setting sun, a cheap copper band twinkling on her arm. She rolled her hips suggestively toward him. A week ago, he would have seen desire in those hips. Today, he saw only her eyes: bored and disinterested, with a hint of loathing.

Lost in thought, Grug passed through the last of the markets, where tables sported fish of nearly every shape, size, and colour, and merchants maintained a competitive banter aimed as much at keeping themselves amused as it was securing customers. At the edge of the district, Grug found himself standing in front of a yellow, stone building that he must have passed hundreds of times before, but never entered. Though the building's face was plain brick, the roof was a mass of inverted arches, crescents balancing seamlessly on one another—it must be gnomish or dwarven work, Grug thought. He followed the lines, his mind working through how each arch balanced the weight of another and, in turn, was balanced. A thick, silver circle stood affixed to the spot the arches came together near the building's front—the symbol of the High Lord.

Strangely compelled, Grug stepped into the church. The floor was simple river stones, the walls bare but for rude, metal candle holders. A small platform rose at the front of the room, a lectern atop it, and a silver circle built into the stonework of the wall behind. Grug strode down the centre aisle, past the short wooden pews, and stood quietly before the platform, his eyes tracing the silver circle again and again as it glowed softly with reflected candle light.

"My son?" The voice was mild, yet deep and comforting. "May I help?"

Grug turned. The priest looked older than his voice suggested, his face weathered by time and sun. As he walked closer, his hand gently skimmed along the tops of the pews, more like a man greeting beloved pets than one in need of support. His white robe, belted with plain hemp robe, brushed the floor softly with his passage.

"I don't know if anyone can help me, Father."

The priest's eyes twinkled. "So say all who come to the High Lord, at first. So said I, once. Come. Sit." He sat in the front pew, gesturing for Grug to do the same. "What is it that troubles you?"

"Everything, Father. Everything has changed." Grug sighed.

The priest smiled knowingly. "All things change, my son. But often when we feel that everything has changed around us, we are the ones who have changed."

"That's just it, Father. Not a week ago I thought of nothing but the moment I was in, the pleasures I could find, the glory I could win. Now...now everything is...different. It's like I've gone mad. I know things I never knew before and I understand things that I never would have even guessed at. I see what people really mean when they speak, even if I don't know the language and I somehow know how they feel. Sometimes, I even know when something is about to happen, and I hear bones rattle like death itself is approaching. But at the same time, I find I can't remember a thing about my past, Father. It's like everything I've ever done has been a story, or a dream that I can't quite catch hold of after I wake. Father, I fear I may have been taken by a demon."

To Grug's surprise, the priest burst into laughter. Grug stood, indignant, and strode toward the door.

The priest's laughter trailed off. "Wait, my son. Please."

Grug, embarrassed and angry, continued to stomp toward the door, his boots clattering on the stones.

"Hold!" The word was a cracking whip, a sergeant's voice, not a priest's. Grug's legs halted, as though of their own volition, and he turned in surprise.

The priest's face was stern, but the laughter still twinkled in his eyes. "I'm sorry, my son. I shouldn't have laughed. Please, come back."

For a moment, Grug hesitated, stubbornly wishing he could stride out of the church and back into the street, but he had nowhere else to go; he had no idea how he could even find the rest of his party, and no one else outside of it that he could confide in. Reluctantly, he walked back and sat down in the pew, the wood creaking gently in protest at his return.

After a moment, the priest nodded in thanks, and spoke. "You are not touched by a demon, my son. Far from it. In fact, I believe you may blessed by the High Lord himself."

Grug stared incredulously at the old man. "This doesn't feel like a blessing."

The old man chuckled. "I bet it doesn't. It certainly didn't for me."

"You?" Grug replied. "This happened to you?"

"Most of the High Lord's priests are not born to the cloth. I certainly was not." He settled back in the pew, his eyes distant. "I was a mercenary. A sword for hire." He grinned wolfishly. "And I was good at it, too. I fought with the Golden Sons in wars across the continent, and over the seas, as well. We fought for whoever was paying—human, dwarf, even drow once; it made no difference to us. It was all glory and gold."

"You fought with the Sons?"

"Twelve years. Longer than most. By the time I left, there were only a handful of my original company left. The rest were dead or retired. I would have retired, but...what would I have done? Killing was the only thing I was good at."

Grug nodded slowly. "But father, I don't see..."

"Patience my son."

The priest drew his robe in tighter around himself. "One day, everything changed. We'd been on a siege contract for weeks. Pretty standard; we mostly stood around while the engineers assembled siege engines and battered the walls. Finally, they ran out of food, and had no choice but to charge from the gates. We cut them to pieces. One unit managed to flank them, slip through the rain of arrows, and jam the gates open."

"We poured in and slaughtered the few defenders that could still fight back. It was pretty clean, for a siege; easy. After the fighting was done, the usual happened: looting; fires; rape. Before we knew it, half the city was in flames and we were pressed into fighting the fires. I think we lost more men to burns and smoke than we had to the archers before we got them all out."

"When the sun rose the next morning, we started dragging bodies out of the rubble. We found..." The priest visibly steeled himself. "We found a passage beneath one of the larger houses. It was full of children. All dead. It might have been an orphanage, perhaps a school; I don't know. But I recognized what was left of the pictures on the walls and the carpets on the floors. I had been in that building to loot, and I remember knocking over a candle. I was rushing through, though, trying to get as much loot as I could before the other soldiers found all of the expensive stuff. I...I had killed them."

"You can't know that," Grug said gently. "Surely there were other fires. I've seen sieges, or at least I think I have; there are always fires."

"Perhaps. But it doesn't really matter. I believe I killed them, in my heart. I resigned the day our contract ended and sold my gear. For almost a year I made my way from tavern to tavern, drinking, dicing, whoring. But every time I closed my eyes I saw those children, blackened."

The silence stretched, as the priest stared into the distance. "Then, one day, I stayed too long in the wrong tavern, was a little bit too free with my coin, and someone decided to take it from me. Three of them, in fact, in the alleyway. By that time, I was too drunk to stand, let alone fight them off. My night ended in blood, trickling away into the gutter. But it was not my time."

"The High Lord came to me, called my name, and told me I had not yet paid for my sins. I followed the sound of church bells to this very church, where the priest found me and tended to my wounds."

"The world looked different to me, after that day. The High Lord opened my eyes and I saw what I had become. Everything changed in an instant, and I couldn't be the same man that I had been. Suddenly, the events of my past seemed distant and remote, like a story I'd read. I could learn from them, but I didn't have to be that man anymore. I was free. Does that sound anything like what has happened to you?"

Grug nodded mutely.

"I thought it might. The High Lord is calling you, my son. He has opened your eyes to the world, and he will expect something in return."

"Do you think he means me to give up my sword?" Grug asked hesitantly.

The priest thought a moment and shook his head. "I don't know.

The High Lord abhors needless violence, and yet violence is a part of life. I have also met some of His paladins, most of whom began as soldiers and mercenaries. I think that when you are ready to follow your path, he will show it to you."

"I'm scared, father," Grug said softly.

The priest took Grug's hand, squeezing it with surprising strength. "I know, my son. So are we all."

For the first time he could remember, Grug Smash began to cry.

CHAPTER 5

THE MORNING AFTER THE NIGHT BEFORE

Morning had come and gone by the time Grug rolled out of his bed in the outer-city inn. His head pounded, and he gulped water from the clay jug on his washstand before lying back down and putting the thin, wool-stuffed pillow over his face to block out the shards of light stabbing into his eyes.

His memory was vague. He remembered leaving the church. He remembered going into the inn's common room and ordering a pitcher of ale. He was pretty sure he could remember ordering the second pitcher. Everything was a bit vague after that.

The soft smell of perfume on his pillow reminded him of how the night had ended—a copper armband glinting in the moonlight as the woman rode him, her back arched and her long, black hair cascading down her back. He remembered, too, her confusion and anger when he told her he wished he could not see her eyes. Light! He hoped he still had his purse...

With a groan, Grug swung his legs over the side of the bed, trying to hold the shattered remnants of his skull together. His stomach pitched and rolled, but he made it to his feet and back to the washstand. Avoiding his red-eyed reflection in the silvered mirror, he picked up his purse; though it was as fat as ever, it gave only the faintest jingle. With a sigh, Grug pulled out a cotton rag from within it and counted the four remaining coppers. At least she had left him enough for breakfast.

Dressing himself was difficult, and putting on his sword belt nearly defeated him. Sweat dripped from his brow as he disentangled his sword from his legs for the third time and firmly knotted the ends of the belt around his waist. Then he sat down and rested for a while.

Finally, the room stopped spinning long enough for Grug to find the door and he got through on only the second try. He navigated the stairs with exaggerated care, clutching the handrail, and was thankful with every step that he had left his axe propped in the corner of his room, lest it spoil what was left of his balance.

The common room was quiet—most had likely had their lunch and left already—but Grug could still smell meat roasting in the kitchen, and the air still carried the faint scent of the morning's bread. His stomach gurgled, something halfway between nausea and hunger, as Grug plunked down at one of the scarred, wooden tables and put his aching head in his hands.

A linen purse hit the top of the table with a clink. Grug looked up with some difficulty at a well-dressed, but unremarkable man of middle years, with short black hair and a well-trimmed goatee. "What's this?"

"The contents of your purse." The man shrugged. "Or most of it, I expect. I probably should have turned the girl upside down and shaken her, but you never know what might have fallen out. May I sit?"

Grug wanted nothing more than to be left alone, but it seemed reasonable courtesy to a man that had just returned what was not an insubstantial amount of money. Grug gestured to a chair and pulled the purse toward him. Sure enough, gold and silver gleamed inside.

"How did you get this? And why?" Grug asked.

"The how is easy. The girl came down the stairs like she had the king's crown beneath her shift, just looking for someone to catch her. As for why...well, it's bad business."

"Whose business?" Grug asked.

The man smiled. "The guild's. The girl doesn't belong to the guild, and we don't like to encourage amateurs to dabble in our business."

Grug raised an eyebrow. "You're a thief."

The man shrugged and smiled again. "I've been called worse. I don't pick a lot of pockets these days, though. I'm more of what you might call...an administrator."

"I'm surprised to see you moving around so early," the barmaid interrupted. "After last night, I didn't think we'd see you down here until after supper." She smiled broadly, showing a missing front tooth. "Not that I'm complaining, mind. Looking for hair of the dog?"

Grug nodded. "Ale, bread, and a cut of whatever meat is cooking, as well. And whatever he wants, too." Grug gestured toward the thief.

The thief smiled. "Tea, please."

The barmaid nodded and left, returning shortly with a tankard and a steaming cup. Grug took a long pull at the tankard before fixing his gaze again on the man across the table. "So. You're a thief—a guild master, if I'm not mistaken—and you retrieved my purse because it's bad business for a non-guild member to be caught thieving. It must keep you awfully busy, tracking down everyone who cuts a purse without paying guild dues."

The thief smiled ruefully. "I admit a certain personal curiosity in this case. It's not all that uncommon a sight to find a barbarian lost in drink and pissing away his gold, but it's a bit more unusual to find one speaking of magic amulets and being chosen by the gods."

It was Grug's turn to be embarrassed. "Oh."

"I wasn't the only one who took note, either. There were plenty of ears that grew a bit longer, if you follow me. I would say the only reason you woke with that necklace still about your neck was that no one was sure they could take it without a bit more planning. Drunk or not, you're a fair-sized fellow."

Grug grunted sourly and nodded in thanks to the barmaid as she set down a platter of gravy-soaked beef and crusty rolls. The ale had begun to settle his stomach, and his head felt only slightly thicker than the table. He broke off half of a roll, dragging it through the thick gravy on the way to his mouth.

"I've put out word within the guild to leave you be, but I would watch your back, if I were you; there's plenty outside the guild that wouldn't mind risking the retribution to claim a prize like that. There are always buyers for magical artifacts, and even if you were exaggerating, you might have quite a rare piece there." He frowned. "It really is an ugly thing, though, isn't it?"

Grug thought that over as he worked his way through the platter in front of him. Finally, he shook his head. "It still doesn't make sense. Curiosity or not, why forbid me to the rest of your own guild? In fact, why wouldn't you be assigning the task of getting the amulet to one of them—especially if you think it's so valuable?"

"Put simply?" the thief said, "Curiosity, I suppose. I've done worse things in its name, before. I'm also looking for some assistance, and I think you might be just the kind of fellow I need."

"Assistance with what?"

"Guild turncoats. Normally, we take care of these things ourselves, but there's something different about this group."

"How so?"

"For one thing, they've managed to eliminate everyone we've sent after them—including members of the assassin's guild. *Senior* members."

Grug's eyebrows lifted. "That would be quite the accomplishment."

The thief nodded, his eyes pensive. "Indeed. They're getting more brazen, as well. They started with cutting purses and robbing nobles—the same sort of thing most of our members do, but without the tithes. We put out word to our own to bring them in, if they could, but we didn't worry over it much. Lately, though, we've been hearing word that they've moved on to extortion, and even abducting people in broad daylight. People say that they grab their target and then disappear in a puff of smoke. It could all be theatrics, but..."

"You don't think so."

"No, I don't. I think either a very talented mage or something worse is helping them."

Grug nodded slowly. "Where are they?"

"The inner city—a nobleman's estate. They've either killed him, or he's part of it; we don't know. You'd have to make it in quietly, or they will just run and find somewhere else to work from." The thief's face grew grim. "These sort are bad for business. We want to make sure they don't come back."

Grug pushed the platter away and leaned back in his chair with a contented sigh. "And what would this little adventure pay?"

"Twenty-five percent of the loot you find, or the guild will top that up to...say...ten gold marks, if they've already fenced everything."

"I don't work alone; I have three others in my party. We'll take 15 percent—each—or fifty gold marks, minimum."

The thief laughed. "You'll have my own guild hiring an assassin for me, if I agree to that. Ten percent each, minimum ten gold marks, if they all know their work, and I'll accompany you myself for another ten percent. The Guild gets half."

"Can you fight?"

With a flourish, the thief spun twin daggers from his sleeves. His eyes never wavered from Grug's as the blades rolled and spun, walking across the backs of his hands in a flash of silver, and slipped back into his sleeves.

Grug grinned. "Done then, but you'll also pay for any equipment we lose or break." He extended a hand across the table.

"Agreed. I'm Samuel, by the way; Samuel Cooper."

"Grug Smash."

Samuel paused. "Really?"

"What do you mean?"

"Your name is Grug...Smash? Fitting for a barbarian warrior, I suppose, but...I don't know; it's almost *too* fitting, don't you think? May I ask where it comes from? Do you have orcish blood, by chance?"

Grug glared indignantly. "No, I do not. My name..." His words trailed off. When he really stopped to think about it, he didn't have any idea where the name came from; it was just his name.

"What were your parents from?"

Grug frowned. "I don't know."

"Are you an orphan?"

"I don't think so."

"How can you not know if you were an orph-"

The inn door opened with a bang, and Bhalon stumped in. His mail suit was brightly burnished and a broad smile lit his face. "Good news, Lad. We've a contract!"

"Bhalon!" Grug exclaimed, "I'm glad to see you! I've got us a contract, as well."

The dwarf looked perplexed. "No time for fancies, Laddie. The thieves guild wants us to track down a bunch of rogue thieves for them."

"But that's what *we* were just talking about," Grug replied, in confusion.

"I told ye, we've no time for fancies," Bhalon said firmly. "The thieves guild master has approached the group and asked us ta help. We're to share ten percent each of the loot, and the guild master himself will accompany us."

Samuel was staring at Bhalon in bafflement. "How did you...who...what the hell is going on?"

"Did you speak with the guild master, or did Haeronor, Bhalon?" Grug asked.

The cleric looked at a loss for words. "I...um...tha' tis, he approached the party...with a quest..." he concluded lamely, his face puzzled.

Grug patted Bhalon fondly on the shoulder. It's okay, Bhalon. Don't worry about it."

The dwarf's confidence returned. "Right. We've got to move now. The guild master will be waiting for us."

Samuel looked like a fish, his mouth opening and closing as he tried to follow what was going on.

Bhalon grabbed Grug's arm and all but dragged him toward the door. Samuel stood, tossed a few coins onto the table for the barmaid, and followed—still looking bewildered.

Grug squinted into the afternoon sunlight as he opened the inn's heavy door. Then he stepped through into pitch black night.

CHAPTER 6

WHISPERS IN THE DARKNESS

"What the bloody hell was that?" Samuel yelped. "Why is it dark?"

"Silence, you fool," Haeronor's voice hissed from the darkness. "Do you want to get us caught?"

Grug's hand came down gently on Samuel's shoulder and his voice whispered softly into his ear: "Let me guess...you were just suddenly here, right?"

"What in the light is going on?"

"It's all right. You get used to it. Just calm down and breathe."

Samuel paused, his shallow, panicked breaths quieting. "Fine. I'm calm," he hissed. "Now what in the nine hells is going on? Where in the light are we?"

"Stop and think. Really think. Can you remember spending the last two days getting ready: watching this house, getting equipment, even climbing the walls to get up here?"

Samuel looked around and saw, as though for the first time, the soaring turrets of the manor house, the paces-wide balcony on which they stood, with a thick, flowing curtain separating it from the main room, and the balustrade at their backs. Beyond the balustrade, the grounds of a noble manor house stretched into the darkness. "Of course I don..." His mouth snapped shut. "Wait...I do, but it's..."

"Vague?" Grug suggested. "Like you read it in a book or someone told you about it?"

"How did you know that?"

Grug's bemused grin was lost to the darkness. "I get that a lot—ever since I found the amulet. I think it happened before that too, though. I just never noticed."

"Then why am I feeling it too?"

Grug paused. "I don't really know. I'm not sure how any of this works."

"That's because it makes no sense, Grug. This isn't a story, it's real life. How could we..." Samuel fumbled for the right words: "skip ahead?"

"It does seem a bit like a story, though, doesn't it? An adventure? It's just that we're the only ones who seem to know about it."

"The others don't feel it too?"

"I don't think they notice; they don't hear the bones clacking, either."

"Bones?"

Grug shrugged, then realized that the thief wouldn't be able to see it in the darkness. "Maybe you'll hear them, too. I don't know what they mean, but they always seem to show up when I'm trying to do something difficult."

"So what should I do in the meantime?"

"Just act normal. Follow the plan—you'll remember, if you really think about it."

Haeronor glared at them through the shadows. "If you two are quite done, we've got sentries to deal with," he whispered.

Grug glided closer to the mage. "Where?"

Haeronor muttered a human detection spell under his breath. The words came slowly and softly; the light from his eyes and hand were similarly muted, barely a glow in the darkness of the balcony. "On top of this wing, heading toward the east wing. If you hurry, you should be able to catch him before he turns back toward us," the mage said, at last. "There's sentry between the north and the east wings, as well."

"Is that all of them, then?"

"All of them on the roofs right now. There are a couple on the edges of the grounds, but unless one of them sees us, and has a blackwood bow, they shouldn't be much trouble. Try not to screw this up and get us all killed, would you?"

Grug held the mage's eyes and tried to ignore the infuriating smirk on his elven face, imagining how much happier he would be to drill his fist into it. At last, he turned away and gestured to Samuel before slipping next to the wall and feeling for handholds. When he looked to see if Samuel was doing the same on the other side of the balcony's opening into the room, the thief was already half way to the roof. Grug hurried to catch up, meeting the thief a few moments later on the top of the broad, slate roof.

"This way," Grug said softly. "Watch for loose tiles."

Samuel grinned. "I have done this before, you know." He set off across the tiles, setting a pace that Grug struggled to match while remaining quiet.

The pair heard the sentry before he came into view. Though the man had forgone a torch, in order to preserve his night vision, his boots clattered on the tiles, with no attempt made to muffle them. Grug and Samuel moved in quickly behind the man, staying on top of the roofline and out of his line of sight. When they got close, Samuel slipped ahead on silent feet, drawing his long dagger when he was mere steps from the man, in order to avoid the blade flashing in the moonlight. With a practiced hand, the thief stepped forward as he swung, the dagger's pommel catching the sentry on the temple.

Grug squatted next to Samuel, wordlessly drawing a length of cord from his pouch and tying the man's hands and feet together. Samuel cut a long strip from the man's tunic, wadded up another piece, and gagged him for good measure. The two nodded to each other and started quietly down the length of the roof, headed toward the north wing of the mansion.

"Is Haeronor always like that?" Samuel asked in a whisper.

"What do you mean?"

"He really doesn't like you, does he?"

"Oh. I'm not sure Haeronor likes *anyone.* Not any humans, anyway."

"Why? Some terrible and tragic event in his past?" Samuel asked.

"Not that I know of. I think he's just a horse's ass."

Samuel snorted.

"Some of it seems to be an elf thing, though. Triwathon doesn't like most humans, either. The feeling is usually mutual," Grug said.

"Fair enough. How did you all end up in a group, then? It doesn't seem terribly likely that two high elves that don't like humans would end up partnering with one, much less a dwarf *and* a human."

Grug paused for a moment. "I don't really remember, actually...One day we just...formed a party. Our skills kind of complemented each other, and it just made sense, I guess."

"So what did you do before that?"

Grug shook his head sadly. "I have no idea. I don't really remember anything before I started adventuring. I think I was a sailor, once, and a pirate, but it's all so vague."

Samuel looked over at Grug for a long moment. "More of that story feeling?"

"Yeah. Something like that."

The two fell silent as they neared the north wing. Before long, they could hear steps shuffling over the roof tiles, coming toward them. Samuel slipped toward the edge of the roof and peered downward. After a moment, he backtracked the way they had come for a few strides, gestured to Grug, and slid down off of the roof. Grug followed silently, peering down to where Samuel waited on a balcony projecting out from the floor below them. He slipped over the edge, and the two waited against the side of the building while the steps above them passed over and beyond before quietly levering themselves back up over the eave and creeping up behind the sentry. This time it was Grug who moved forward, standing to his full height and slipping one muscled arm around the sentry's throat. The man thrashed and reached for his sword, but Grug's hand was already there, enveloping the man's wrist while he dragged him backward to the ground. Grug squeezed until the man's eyes lost focus and he went limp.

Samuel checked quickly to see the man was breathing, and gagged him while Grug tied his hands and feet. The two crouched quietly for a moment, listening for any sign that another sentry had heard the noise, or seen their silhouettes against the night sky. When no signs came, they slowly made their way back along the roof toward the rest of the party.

"It's nice being out again," Samuel said after they had walked along in silence for a bit.

"What do you mean?" Grug asked.

"As guild master, I generally just oversee things, keep track of the jobs everyone else is working on, and ensure that all the dues are properly paid. I'm good at it, and it's valuable, but it's not often exciting. It's nice to be out in the night air being a proper scoundrel again."

They arrived back at the balcony where the rest of the part waited, just outside of the chambers that Haeronor had said the rogue thieves were using as a meeting spot. Grug wondered for a moment how exactly Haeronor had found that out; sure enough, somewhere in his vague recollection of their preparations was a conversation between Haeronor and Bhalon about how the mage had used an eavesdropping spell of some kind to pick the information out. Grug pondered briefly if another mage would be able to sense Haeronor's spells, as he slipped over the edge of the eave and down the wall.

"Haeronor?" Grug asked, "would another mage..."

"Quiet!" Haeronor hissed. "Here they come."

Flickers of torch light peeked through the arrow slits in the turret, winding their way ever closer to the open room and the balcony beyond, where Grug and his party were perched. Grug kept his eyes trained on the darkened room, scanning the inner courtyard occasionally to keep an eye out for patrolling guards or archers.

"I still think it's stupid," a soft, fluting voice whined. "We should have just knifed him and taken his purse."

Grug watched the torch move behind the curtain separating the balcony from the main room, silhouetting a second man and giving him the size of a giant. There was a fleshy thud, like a body hitting the ground, and a muffled cry.

“Darathan wants to see him,” rasped a second man. “Do you want to be the one to tell him you knifed him instead, because carrying him back would be too much trouble?”

“No,” came the sulky reply, “but I still think...”

“You're not being paid to think, are you? Now shut up and light the torches. Darathan should be here soon.”

Grug felt himself shrink back toward the balcony rail as the light grew inside the room, though he knew that night blindness would make it almost impossible to see them, even if one of the thieves peeked through the curtain. He wondered briefly if that had to do with how eyes seemed to shrink in response to light and the time it took for them to grow back to a size that could absorb enough of the dim light to see reflections off of other objects. “Maybe it would be better to just be a dumb barbarian,” Grug muttered. “I understood my axe, at least.” Grug absently started calculating how much force was applied at the end of his axe, relative to the length of its handle, the strength of his swing, and the weight of the axe head.

Another torch began to wind its way up the turret staircase toward the room, and the men within grew quiet. Triwathon slid carefully closer to the curtain, his soft leather shoes whispering beneath him. Slipping quietly to his belly at the corner of the opening, he peered beneath the curtain and into the room beyond.

Grug watched the elf's hand signals. Three men: two warriors, one captive. The newcomer was also male, and not obviously armed.

A man's voice, booming like an orator, made Grug jump: “You idiots! What in the eternal fires did you think you were doing? I've heard half a dozen reports already about the nephew of the king being captured, in the middle of a bloody tavern!”

"You said you wanted it handled quickly," the second man complained. "No one will have seen our faces with all the smoke."

"Yeah," the whiny voice piped up. "It was you that was in the hurry."

"You keep your sniveling mouth shut, or I'll have your tongue," the newcomer growled.

"It's fine, Darathan," the second man said soothingly. "Yorik will keep his mouth shut, and one way or the other, you have the man you were looking for."

The silence stretched. "We will speak of this later," Darathan finally replied. Footsteps echoed off the stone floor as he stalked to the other side of the room. "My lord," he said sarcastically, "how good of you to join us. I've so looked forward to making your acquaintance."

A sputtering announced that a gag had been removed. "You will hang for this." The voice was cultured, but the tone was sharpened steel—a promise, not a threat.

"I'd be more careful, if I were you. I'm a patient fellow, but my friends here tend to be a little more...violent."

"You know, you may be right about that," the raspy-voiced man agreed. "I think violent would be the perfect word for us."

Grug could hear the wicked grin in the man's voice, but the captive seemed un-phased. "You can be patient, violent, or bloody drow for all the difference it will make. You'll not get whatever it is you're looking for from me."

"Oho!" Darathan boomed. "A brave one, boys! How fun! But we don't have to be that way, do we? We're just looking for a few answers...just a bit of information about your uncle, the King."

There was the wet sound of someone spitting, and a soft splatter as it hit the floor. Darathan chuckled dangerously. "Oh, my boy. You have no idea how happy that makes me. I just love a challenge."

Triwathon began to sign again, his movements quick and panicked, and his eyes darting back to meet Haeronor's. Grug caught something about a circle, but couldn't see the rest for the speed and the gloom. Rhythmic chanting had begun to pulse from the room, rising and falling like a waves crashing against the shoreline. Though Grug couldn't understand the words, he felt them crawl across his body like grave worms.

Clearly, Haeronor felt the same, or whatever Triwathon had signed was urgent enough. "Now!" the mage screamed, throwing himself toward the curtain. "We must stop him before..." Haeronor broke off with a strangled cry that every member of the party echoed as they pushed through the curtain. Standing in a circle of salt nearly five feet wide, was a being Grug could only call a demon.

CHAPTER 7

A DARKER PLOT EMERGES

The party skidded to a halt, their feet stopping as though of their own volition. The demon was tall—nearly ten feet, Grug guessed—and his (it was definitely, and impressively male) shoulders stood wide enough to span the circle. Horns and spikes sprouted across his forehead and rode down the slope of his neck to his shoulders, and his red skin steamed in the cold night air. Heavy, clawed hands flexed at the end of impossibly long arms, nearly scraping the floor. Then the demon's eyes opened and Grug looked into a circle of hell.

"So kind of you to join us," Darathan drawled. "I had begun to wonder if you were going to lounge around on the balcony all night." He gave the party a condescending smile. "Or wander about on the roof. Interesting choice to bind them, rather than killing them, by the way. I wouldn't have expected that from a barbarian and a thief. Normally your kind is all about swinging a big sword—or a blade in the dark."

"I prefer an axe," Grug said. "More weight for the chopping."

"Well, you're the professional in that area," the sorcerer replied. "I'll take your word for it."

"I'd be pleased to demonstrate."

"Cheeky," the sorcerer said with a smile. "I like that. You'll serve me well."

"No," Grug said matter of factly, "I won't."

"But you already have, by bringing that amulet to me. Thank you, by the way; it really is a rare piece. The power it can lend to someone versed in the arts is truly...remarkable." His gaze flicked to Haeronor: "I'm surprised you didn't take it for yourself, little mage."

Haeronor managed to look embarrassed and furious all at once. Bhalon looked like a thunderhead ready to split open with fury. "This was all a trick, then? A deception to bring the lad closer to ye?"

"Oh, no," Darathan replied. "This is quite real, I assure you. With that amulet at my disposal and a little bit of information from our friend here," he said, casually kicking the captive beneath the ribs, "it should be a simple matter to put myself on the throne."

"The people with never accept you!" the captive gasped.

"No? And what if I look, sound, and even act like the king? I'm sure his favourite nephew must know *something* of his mannerisms, yes? That amulet will give me the power to hold the spells almost indefinitely. Standing against me will be seen as treason; no one opposes the king."

"High Lord protect us," Bhalon whispered.

The captive went pale. "You rotten bastard! You won't get away with this!"

Darathan laughed. "And who's to stop me? The only people who have any idea it's happening are in this room. Your family will be *so* disappointed when you return, mad and broken. And as for you five...well, soon your own interests will be so aligned with my own that you wouldn't dream of getting in my way." The sorcerer spoke in a guttural tongue that rasped across Grug's skin like a file, and left him feeling sickened and defiled. The demon roared in anger and pain as a cord the colour of dried blood solidified out of the air, tethering it to the sorcerer. Darathan drew deeply from the demonic well he had summoned, his face and neck flushing with power, and his eyes rolling ecstatically in their sockets.

Grug and Bhalon stepped forward in unison, raising their weapons, but a wave of power struck them, dropping them to their knees. Grug looked up at the sorcerer and felt his soul torn to pieces.

*   *   *

Haeronor stood on a dais, looking down at the scores of disciples and initiates that thronged the great hall of the Tree and Leaf order. To his left, the initiates of the purple robe, his former order, stood, many with looks of bitterness and anger poorly hidden under false smiles. Haeronor reveled in their jealousy, barely containing a smirk as he looked their way. Initiates from the other orders—blue, orange, and grey—stood in their clusters around the hall, surrounded by throngs of black robed disciples. His. All of them were his, now.

Haeronor smoothed the front of his opulent white, silk robes with pleasure as he took his place at the lectern. He paused for a moment, drawing eyes and letting the last murmurs of conversation cease. "My children," he began, "it is with the greatest pride that I don the white mantle this morning. When I joined the order, over a decade ago, I dreamed of one day rising to the office of archmage. I burned for it. I studied hard, delving into realms of magic that many of you will never dream of entering, and seeking lore that may be as dangerous to those that find it, as it is to their enemies. Never did I falter. And now I stand before you."

Haeronor paused while the disciples cheered. He was delighted to note that some of the purple robes looked about to be sick. Braithwait, his most difficult teacher and a staunch disciplinarian, was red-faced and indignant, puffed up like a toad. Haeronor couldn't contain his mirth, and broke into delighted laughter. "Thank you, all!"

"Archmage." A curiously robed mage stood to one side of the podium, the archmage's golden chain of office in his hands. "It is time for the investiture. Once the chain of office is upon you, you will be archmage in law, as well as custom. All you have to do is put it on."

Haeronor stepped forward with a smile on his face, but a heavy rumble shook the room. Haeronor jumped back in surprise, looking around the room, but no one else seemed to have noticed the sound. He stepped forward again, and a second rumble nearly threw him from his feet. When Haeronor peered toward the back of the room, a silver light emerged from the walls and doorways, swallowing up initiates and disciples alike. Before he could think of a spell to cast, it enveloped him.

* * *

The room was dark when Samuel awoke. He guessed it was past midnight, still hours away from dawn. The room was cold; it was still too early in the fall for his father to begin stocking the stove at night, but too late for any hope of a warm summer night.

Samuel threw the blankets back and stepped cautiously onto the floor, wincing as the cold tiles sent a shiver from the soles of his feet through the top of his head. He paused a moment, listening intently and trying to think what might have woken him, but the house was quiet. Even the cats had long since finished chasing their prey and settled into their beds—or onto his, he thought with a smile, as he stroked Blackie's warm dark coat. The cat purred deep in its chest, stretching its legs up in front of its nose, and promptly fell back asleep.

Samuel padded silently into the kitchen, nearly tripping over a second cat, who clearly thought the middle of the night was a perfectly reasonable time to be fed. When he looked up, there was a willowy, dark-haired woman standing on the other side of the room, near the stove. "Mother?"

The woman smiled broadly, her eyes sparkling and full of joy. "Samuel! What are you doing up so late?"

"I thought I heard...I mean...maybe the cats... What are you doing up?"

"Oh, nothing important. Just getting ready for the day, sweetheart."

"But it isn't even dawn yet."

"Yes, well, perhaps we should both be getting back to bed, then. What do you think?"

"I suppose," Samuel said slowly. Something was wrong, but he couldn't quite put his finger on it. His brain seemed caught in a fog.

"You're just sleepy, dear," his mother said. "Why don't you give me a hug, and go back to sleep?"

Samuel started to shuffle forward automatically, but a clang like a blacksmith at the world's biggest forge shook the room. "What was that?"

"It was nothing," his mother snapped. "Now come give me a hug and get back to bed."

A second rumbling clang shook the room. Silver mist boiled from the woodstove, and the world began to fade. The last thing Samuel saw was a look of anger and frustration in his mother's eyes.

*　　*　　*

Triwathon leapt gracefully over the gigantic dorvakin, to great cheers from the crowd. The dorvakin's claws, twice as long as Triwathon's fingers, dug into the grass, soil, and even the rock below, spinning it back to face the elf. Three mouths, overflowing with razor-sharped teeth, snapped at Triwathon as the animal bounded back into the fray. Triwathon rolled out of the way at the last moment, stretching out on the ground with his head leaned onto his hand, and one leg crooked lazily over the other.

The crowd went wild. Men yelled their incredulity, while women screamed his name. Triwathon loved every moment.

Flipping up to his feet, Triwathon effortlessly dodged the dorvakin's next attack and drew his bow, firing high into the air. Hunkering down as though playing with his favourite dog, the ranger baited his prey, goading the dorvakin closer. It approached somewhat cautiously, frustrated at its failure to catch the infuriating man and agitated from the roar of the crowd.

With a whistle, the arrow returned from the sky, burying itself in the animal's back. The dorvakin roared and arched, rolling to remove the barbed shaft from its back. Triwathon played to the crowd, using the animal's distraction to set out five arrows in the turf before him. As the dorvakin charged, Triwathon sprang into action, firing all five arrows in the space of heartbeats, punching through the animal's tough hide, and into its vital parts, with the final arrow puncturing its heart. Staggered, the animal tried to keep its feet, watching Triwathon with hatred and loathing as he stood gloating to the crowd. Darkness closed over its eyes.

An elven maiden, her dress and jewels declaring her part of the royal family, stepped forward from the crowd. "You've conquered the beast, ranger. Come and claim your prize."

Triwathon grinned and strutted triumphantly across his field of victory. He was only paces from the maiden when a rumble like thunder resounded across the glade, the pure cry of metal meeting stone, with a force that made his heart skip in his chest. For a moment, the smile on the maiden's face slipped, her eyes glittering in fury, before disappearing so quickly that Triwathon was sure he must have imagined it. A second shockwave took Triwathon in the back, and he turned to see the body of the dorvakin dissolving into silvery mist. He stepped toward it, stretching out his hand in wonder, and was consumed.

* * *

Grug sat at a table in the inn's common room, his back to the fire. The wood beneath his fingers was faintly sticky, and the air smelt of beer and sweat. He was home.

The room was crowded, nearly full, with strangers packed in at every table but his. Grug sipped his ale and watched as more and more people came in the inn door. Some glanced his way, considering the empty seats around his table, but no one sat. They wandered off to the periphery of the room, sitting if they could find a seat, and standing where they couldn't, drinking and talking genially amongst themselves.

Grug felt a pang of loneliness that cut to his core. He tried to hold it off, telling himself the only friends he needed were in the cup in front of him and in a sheath at his side, but the emptiness within him grew. He gestured to the seats at his table when the next group of people shuffled in the door, but they sneered at him and squeezed into the press of bodies that were now stacked tight as cord wood along the walls and between the tables.

“Barbarian.”

Grug looked over to the next table where another man also sat alone; Grug wondered how he could have missed seeing him before. He was older, clearly a northerner himself, and covered in both weapons and scars.

“Come; sit,” the older man said, gesturing to the chair next to him.

Grug sprang to his feet and took hold of his tankard, taking a place at the man's table. Grug's table disappeared behind him in a mass of bodies, like a high tide engulfing a reef.

The man nodded in greeting and smiled. "A fellow adventurer, eh? Well, you're certainly welcome at my table! What's your name, boy?"

"Grug," Grug replied. "Grug Smash."

"A fine name," the old man boomed. "Fit for the north, I'd say. I'm Einar." He held out one meaty hand.

Grug noticed how the last two fingers on the man's hand curled inward, as though he'd held a sword too long. When he shook his hand, though, it was soft, almost delicate, as though it belonged to a completely different man than the one in front of him. Grug shook off a vague sense of unease.

"And where are you headed?" Einar asked. "Are you hiring out, or are you already contracted?"

"Nothing at the moment," Grug replied. "I expect I'll hear something in the next tenday or so."

Einar leaned back in his chair and gave Grug a considering look. "You know, I may have just the job for you. It shouldn't take too long, and the pay isn't great, but the company is good." He grinned. "It would be nice to have another barbarian in the group. It gets a little lonely being the only northerner sometimes, doesn't it?"

Somewhere in the back of Grug's mind, something screamed for his attention, but he found himself nodding. "Sure. I'll come along."

"Great," Einar bellowed, throwing back the last of his ale and pushing his chair back. "Let's go." He began pushing his way toward the door.

As Grug moved to follow, the room shook like it was in the centre of an earthquake, and a deafening metallic clang sent Grug's hands to his ears. "What in the nine hells was that?"

Einar looked annoyed. "It was nothing. Come on; we're going to be late." He started back toward Grug, but the room shuddered again, and a second clang staggered him back. His face erupted in rage.

A silvery mist coiled out of the fireplace and ate the nearest tables, people and all. It sprang forward, catching Grug's ankle and pulling sharply. He fell, expecting to crash into the wooden floor of the common room, but landed instead on a soft cushion of air that cocooned around him and held him safe at its heart.

* * *

The metal cage was no more than two feet square, with iron points on the floor, distanced enough to stand between, but not enough to lay down and rest. Bhalon hunched within, elbows braced on knees, looking out between the iron strapping to where the demon stood, sharpening its knives and hooks. Behind it, a black altar rose from the stone floor as though part of the granite itself, stained with the blood of a thousand victims. A hearth, twice the height of the altar, roared with flames, and, improbably, screams.

The demon grinned, pointed black teeth grating together with a sound like metal dragged edge over edge, screeching up and down Bhalon's spine. "It's been a long time since I've had dwarf meat," the demon growled. "Even longer since I've dined on a disciple of the Foe."

Bhalon's throat was dry and parched, but he croaked as best he could: "May ye' choke on me, ye' rotten bastard."

The demon chuckled. "So fierce, little cleric. So brave and sure of your lord's favour. How then do you find yourself here? Where is your savior now?"

Bhalon glared but said nothing. He turned inward instead, for the hundredth time since he'd found himself bound here, he thought, and found only emptiness. The centre of love and strength that had always lain at his core was gone, as though it had never been. He fought to keep his face straight, his tears unshed at finding himself so horribly alone.

The demon smiled gruesomely. “I can smell your pain, cleric. You can't hide it. Your body slowly cripples itself, and your spirit breaks. It doesn't have to, though. You are choosing it, choosing to break yourself.”

The demon reached into the fire and grabbed a length of iron, its end glowing yellow with heat. He walked over to the cage, and stuck the iron through, pushing it toward the Bhalon with exaggerated slowness, letting the dwarf anticipate the feeling of the hot metal long before it seared into his flesh.

Bhalon screamed, his eyes streaming and his knees buckling. He slammed into the spikes at the bottom of the iron cage, slashing and puncturing his skin and soft tissues; he shot back up, slamming his head into the iron ceiling and cursing in a messy mixture of English and Dwarvish.

“That's it, cleric,” the demon said. “Embrace that hatred. Let me into your heart.”

Bhalon snapped his mouth shut so hard that his teeth clacked together and felt liable to splinter. Despair rode him, fought to take his mind and his heart, and the demon smiled his terrible smile, promising an eternity of pain and servitude.

“You will break,” the demon said conversationally. “And then I will take the rest of your party into the fires. You will emerge only to do my bidding; my horsemen, to ride and spread hatred and discord. Your souls will be mine.

Bhalon thought of Grug, enslaved to a demon, Haeronor and Triwathon doing its bidding and trapped eternally in its torments. “No,” he said hoarsely.

“What was that?” the demon asked.

"I said 'no,' devil-spawn. Ye' may no' have them. For a moment, Bhalon felt a soft touch at his back. He grinned at the demon.

The demon's smile fell. "I will destroy your body!" he cried, desperately.

Bhalon nodded. "Aye. Ye' may. But no' my faith." Silver light blazed from his eyes, and he thrust his hand forth to pull a glowing, silver hammer from the air before him.

The demon bellowed in anger, as Bhalon crashed through the bars enclosing them as though they were twigs. The dwarf rose to his full height, righteous anger pouring from him in silver waves that staggered the demon and suffocated the flames in the great hearth. Bhalon raised the hammer high and brought it crashing into the granite altar, which rang like an enormous bell, shaking the room. With a savage grin, the dwarf swung again, and the altar shattered, black granite exploding out toward the demon, and embedding in its twisted, red flesh.

The room vanished in a cloud of silver.

* * *

Grug opened his eyes just in time to see Darathan thrown back, narrowly missing the demon, and skidding to a stop beyond. The sorcerer seemed dazed, and the demon was down on one knee, as though exhausted.

Bhalon began to laugh. The sound seemed impossible, ridiculous in a room where a sorcerer and a demon stood, doing their best to kill or subjugate them, but Bhalon persevered. The hoarse chuckle turned to peals of laughter that threw the sorcerer's hate back in his face.

"Ye canno' beat us like tha'" Bhalon said. "We will never serve ye'."

Darathan rose to his feet, his eyes and hands swallowed by an inky blackness. "If I cannot have your service, I *will* take your lives," he boomed. "I will strip the flesh from your—"

A deep growl interrupted him. All eyes turned to the demon, which was gently pushing his foot through a break in the salt circle, as though testing unknown waters. Darathan stared in horror at the space where he had slid through the salt as the demon stepped over the scattered crystals and into the world beyond the circle.

"You fool!" Darathan screamed at Grug. "The binding spell has not yet been laid upon it! You've doomed us all!"

The sorcerer's words ended in a screech as one red arm lashed out, far faster than Grug could have imagined for a beast so large, grabbing the sorcerer by the front of his robes and drawing him toward a gaping maw full of serrated, black teeth. A sudden flash and a sulphurous puff of smoke announced the mage's escape, and black teeth closed on nothing but cloth. An unearthly bellow broke from the demon's crimson lips, as he voiced his anger to the night.

The whiny thief began backing slowly toward the staircase, pulling at the other thief's sleeve. "Come on Horatio," he whispered, the whine in his voice turning to desperation, "let's get the hell out of here!"

Before he could take another step, the demon's other arm had shot out, grabbing him around the torso. This time, there was no puff of smoke, only meaty, crunching sounds as the demon bit the thief's head from his neck. Ignoring the bloody spray, the demon threw the body aside, still crunching as he appraised the party arrayed in front of him. The second thief used the moment to quietly slip out of the room.

At last, the demon spoke, his voice like boulders crashing down a cliff: "The Foe may have protected you from the sorcerer, tiny man, but He cannot protect you from *me*."

Bhalon's lips pulled back in a snarl of his own. "I'll put my trust in the High Lord, hellspawn. And it's *dwarf,* ya black-hearted bastard!" Rearing back, Bhalon threw his hammer. It soared through the air, its aim unwavering, but the demon brushed it aside contemptuously. It crashed through a column and disappeared in a flash of light.

"You speak of hearts. I will feast on yours."

Grug felt more than saw the demon move forward, and time seemed to slow. Triwathon threw himself to the side of the room, an arrow leaping from the string of his bow. His arm was reaching back for a second arrow even before the string had come to rest, and he loosed again as he swiftly moved into a flanking position.

Haeronor glowed golden, and Grug could feel a gentle tugging at his mind as a spell was cast. The magic missile burst on the demon's chest; a second and third missile quickly followed.

Neither arrows nor magic did more than slow the demon, but it was enough.

Bhalon glowed like silver sun, his radiant light eclipsing Haeronor's and shining like a beacon throughout the room, without casting a single shadow. The demon skidded to a halt, throwing its clawed hands in front of its eyes and filling the room with an unholy screeching. Bhalon advanced, his chanted prayers to the High Lord weaving a counterpoint to the demon's cries.

The monster roared in pain, clawed feet skittering on the floor tiles as it backed further away from the party, slowly crossing the broken salt line. Grug lurched toward the low table at the side of the room, scooping up a short clay pot still part-way full of salt and preparing himself to close the circle again.

As Grug turned, the march of silver light faltered. Bhalon's eyes were wide and crimson bloomed on his chest. The greater length of a yard-long arrow stood out from his back, its broad head pushing against the inside of Bhalon's hauberk. The party stopped, staring in horror at the dwarf and the demon, which was carefully lowering its claws from in front of its eyes. A low, furious roar shook the room to its stone foundations, and suddenly time sped up again. Grug threw himself into Bhalon, knocking the cleric to the floor only moments before razor sharp claws cut through the air where his head would have been.

Swinging the wounded dwarf onto his shoulder, Grug slipped his axe back into its belt loop, turned and ran toward the doorway. Haeronor and Triwathon loosed spell and arrow to cover their retreat, drawing the demon onto the balcony, and away from Grug.

Clattering down the stone steps of the turret, Grug could still hear the heavy thudding of the demon's feet on the floor above; he ran faster.

With elven speed and grace aiding them, Haeronor and Triwathon slid down a heavy coiled rope from the balcony above, landing just as Grug burst from the turret door and started pounding his way across the inner courtyard. Above, the demon bellowed its fury to the night and hunched in on itself, the heavy red leather of its back bulging and splitting gruesomely apart to unveil thick, bat-like wings. The stone hissed in protest as dark blood and mucus dripped down onto them, etching tiny rivers and streams. Grug looked over his shoulder in time to see the mighty wings flex, spattering the balcony with gore, as the demon launched itself into the night. The barbarian hesitated for only a moment to wonder if Samuel and the king's nephew had made it out alive before he turned and ran as fast as his legs could carry him.

CHAPTER 8

A HANDFUL OF SALT

Grug's breath blew hoarsely from his open mouth as he ran, dodging from building to building, with one eye on the dark sky. Leathery wing beats seemed to echo all around him, and his heart lurched at every movement, real or imagined, that he saw in the night. Grug's shoulder burned where Bhalon's armour had rubbed it raw, and he wished fervently that he dared risk leaving the dwarf behind—but the demon's ability to smell the High Lord's blessing on him made it all but certain that the demon would hunt Bhalon down, for sport if not for spite.

The streets were all but deserted, with most honest people long abed. Those the party did pass needed little encouragement beyond the look on Grug's face and Bhalon's unconscious form to go back indoors and bar their door against the night.

Haeronor and Triwathon ran alongside Grug, keen elven eyes scouting the darkened streets at each stop and hands flickering in the signed language that Grug had never followed on past missions, but which he now seemed to understand. “Clear. Cross left. Stables,”

Triwathon signed quickly, and Haeronor motioned Grug forward toward a large wooden building that smelled of hay and animals.

Inside, Grug followed Haeronor's brisk instructions, laying Bhalon on the side opposite the arrow. Brow furrowed and eyes glowing softly, the mage drew a golden finger down the length of the dwarf's armour, pulling it carefully to the side as the links parted. Another soft touch burned the shaft of the arrow away a few fingers from Bhalon's back so that the mail could be pulled over top of it. Still unconscious, Bhalon sighed in relief.

Haeronor gently traced the wounds on Bhalon's chest and back and the blood slowed to a trickle. "There's little else I can do here," the mage whispered, shaking his head. "If I remove the arrow, I may not be able to stop the bleeding." He carefully pulled Bhalon's knee forward so the dwarf could rest on his side comfortably. Moving to Bhalon's head, Haeronor laid his hands on it and closed his eyes.

Grug started as a sleek shadow rubbed against his leg. His sword was half from its sheath when the soft glow from Haeronor's hands revealed a big, black barn cat, already rumbling a friendly purr deep in its chest. Despite Bhalon's plight, despite his own, Grug smiled and scratched behind the cat's ears. Haeronor's muffled chanting stopped and he stood to his full height, eyes distant and his nostrils flared. "Smoke," he whispered.

Triwathon dropped from the hayloft soundlessly, his eyes wide with fear. "Run, you fools," he whispered fiercely. "We have been found!"

The wall of the stable imploded, showering them with smoking fragments of wood, hay, and manure. Grug turned away to save his eyes, twisting his body to block the door of the stall where Bhalon lay, as best he could.

The demon strode in through the remains of the stable wall, hay scorching and smoking beneath his clawed feet.

Haeronor hummed with power and the mage's eyes blazed as he stepped past Grug and placed himself in front of where Triwathon lay motionless, knocked unconscious or killed by the debris. Lightning sizzled from Haeronor's fingers, arcing across the demon's chest. Magic missiles and firedarts followed, slamming into the monster and driving him back into the stable yard. Grug and Haeronor followed, emerging from the hole in the barn wall into a cloud of smoke and ozone. Without a word, the warrior and the mage spread out, flanking the beast that was now slowly climbing to its feet.

A gravelly chuckle turned to peals of guttural laughter, as the demon stood again to face them. "Puny mage!" the demon spat. "Is this what magic has come to? Is this truly the best you can do?" He lifted one clawed foot high into the air, slamming it back to the ground. The shockwave tossed Grug and Haeronor like rag dolls; only years of training kept Grug's hand tight on the hilt of his sword. "You are not even worth my efforts," the demon roared. "My children will devour you." It scraped one long claw across its palm, shaking thick, black blood onto the ground. Where the blood landed, the soil hissed and writhed as though in agony; steaming, black cesspools whirled and stretched up to the night sky, as fresh blood demons wriggled their way into existence.

When Grug rose to his feet, he faced nine foes, each an emaciated, faceless black mass. Flickers of light from the now-burning stable wall played off inky black skin that flowed like water across the surface of each demon, while elastic ropes of demonic flesh rose and fell from each body, searching, scenting, exploring the air around it for a foe. At some unseen signal, the demons started forward, dark claws forming on the ends of shapeless hands, ropes lashing like angry snakes in their wake.

Every fiber in him roiling in revulsion, and fighting to keep himself from running screaming into the night, Grug trotted farther into the stable yard, circling around to put the demons between him and the stable, where their darkness best contrasted with the fire's light. The demon closest hissed, its long, forked tongue undulating in his direction, and raised its arm to slash at him. Without slowing, Grug gracefully ducked the blow, bringing his blade across the demon's middle. He grunted in surprise as the blade passed neatly and nearly effortlessly through the demon's slim waist, neatly shearing it two, with a sensation that Grug thought must be like slicing through water.

All of the blood demons paused mid-step, as though connected. With a sucking sound, fleshy ropes extended from the fallen demon's severed torso to where its legs continued to stand. Slowly, with a liquid grace, the torso drew itself back upright, settling back into place with a wet squelch that made Grug's stomach turn.

"Hellfire," the barbarian whispered.

Grug sought the calm center of himself, took a deep breath, and waded into the fray. Inky body parts flew, scattered by his whirling blade, and Grug did what he could to send each limb flying as far from its owner as possible. When he passed through the final rank, Grug turned. With the fire now at his back, he stared into the darkness, doing his best to keep both the greater demon and its denizens in his peripheral vision, relying on the blood demons' movements to give away their position.

Grug's heart sank, as he realized that the blood demons clearly didn't need to recapture their own body parts—any would do. Inky blackness swam across the gritty surface of the stable yard, flowing like tar into larger pools. In some spots, two or three demons began forming into one, until four demons, all larger than the original nine, stood before him.

A fire dart shot above Grug's shoulder, striking one demon in the chest; the dart disappeared in a wisp of steam. A magic missile crashed into one demon's leg, knocking it off balance; new midnight flesh flowed, swiftly filling the void. Then they were upon him.

Grug fought for his life, his mighty sword arcing around him, while Haeronor tried spell after spell against their foes. With a wet smack, one sticky rope curled around Grug's arm, forming sharp barbs that burrowed into his skin. He screamed in pain, desperately stabbing at the blood demon with his dagger, and tearing his own flesh away as he wrenched his arm back. The demon opened wide its many-fanged mouth, and froze in anticipation of its meal to come.

It took Grug a moment to realize that the lips weren't going to close. In fact, even the skin had stopped flowing, and a crystalline dusting of ice crawled its way around the demon, enveloping it. When Grug pulled back again, the ropes around his arm tore free, some crashing in frozen shards to the ground below. In short order, Haeronor had frozen the remaining two, though it left the mage panting and exhausted.

Grug briefly considered shattering the blood demons, but feared that they might melt more quickly, and reform again. Instead, he trudged back to Haeronor's side, eyes all for the demon that stood silently, watching and judging them.

A grotesque chuckle broke from twisted lips. "The end has come for you, little ones, though I have not had a chase like this for centuries. Perhaps I shall keep your souls as playthings to remember it." He nodded toward the stable, now with flames dancing on much of the roof and walls. "All but the cleric." The horrifying face twisted further in loathing and disgust. "He shall burn in the eternal fires of my master this night."

Bones rattling in his head and sword clenched in his fist, Grug Smash stepped forth to meet his doom—and promptly tripped over the barn cat. Cursing his luck, Grug rolled to his feet, the sandy soil of the stable yard clinging to his bloodied arm and sweaty body.

The cat was rigid as stone, fur raised all along its back, and its teeth bared in an angry growl at the demon that had foolishly wandered into its domain. With barely a glance for the barbarian that had tripped over it, the cat began to advance, a deep growl in its chest.

Haeronor looked up exhaustedly, sparing a surprised and pitying glance for the cat stalking past him before being seized with sudden inspiration. Chanting softly, Haeronor filled the cat with a soft, golden glow, slumping to the ground in exhaustion as he released the spell.

For a moment, everything stopped and time seemed to slow for Grug once more; he felt at once completely aware of everything around him. The demon, shimmering globs of black ichor still staining its wings, stared in bewilderment at the hissing feline before it. The cat, remained rigid with fury, eyes locked on at the unnatural creature that had invaded its home. Haeronor lay still in the dirt, clearly pushed to his limit. Grug could only assume that his last attempt at a spell, no matter how inspired, had failed. Behind them, thick black smoke had begun to boil forth from the rear of the stable, heralding fire that would soon consume Bhalon and Triwathon. There seemed nothing for Grug to do except summon his courage and leap into the teeth of his destruction.

Before he could take his first step, the cat began to grow. Its growl became deeper, a bass rumble that Grug could feel in his chest, as the cat expanded to the size of a large dog. Grug stepped back involuntarily as the cat reached the size of the jungle cats he had once heard tales of—and kept growing. The demon seemed to realize his danger when the cat reached the size of a horse and cart, but by that time it was too late. One mighty paw, its claws each the size of a dagger, slammed into the red and black chest, sending the demon spinning through the wooden fence encircling the yard, and into the street.

Without a moment's hesitation, the cat leapt over the fence and pounced on his foe. The two rolled on the hard-packed dirt, slamming into the front of the stable, which creaked and swayed alarmingly. Grug could hear an ominous groan in the beams that sang accompaniment to the crackle of flames now engulfing the building's roof.

With little time to spare, Grug sheathed his sword, cursing the black blood that would undoubtedly foul the scabbard, but lacking the time to clean it off. Taking a deep breath, he dashed through the hole in the stable wall, sliding to a stop next to Triwathon's prone form, and heaving him into his arms. Grug staggered out of the building, dropping the elf unceremoniously next to his kin, and ran back into the stable. Hay was burning everywhere, the interior of the stable boiling with smoke and hot ash that burned Grug's skin and wreaked havoc with his sense of direction. Holding his sweat-soaked armor under-padding over his mouth, Grug took as deep a breath as he dared in the smoke, and kept moving. He found Bhalon, still unconscious, in the stall where he had left him, fortuitously protected from the rain of sparks and ash.

Something heavy crashed into the side of the stable, and the groans of the beams turned to cracking. With one eye on the ceiling above him, which rained down dirt and splinters onto his head, Grug lifted the dwarf gently from the straw. Trying not to disturb the remains of the arrow, Grug cradled Bhalon in his arms and lurched to his feet, exhaustion and the weight of the dwarf's stocky body making him sway precariously. Bhalon muttered something softly, but his eyes remained closed.

With a heavy crash and a whoosh of hot air and ashes that coated Grug's back, the rear section of the stable roof collapsed. Fear lent Grug speed, and he burst out of the stable wall and into the yard, coughing and sputtering as he gasped the night air into his starved lungs. Behind him, more beams cracked as chunks of burning roof rained down into the remains of the building.

Carefully laying Bhalon down next to Haeronor and Triwathon, Grug pulled his sword from its scabbard and the axe from its loop on his belt and inched his way carefully over the remains of the stable fence and into the street. He could see that the monstrous cat and the demon were still locked in combat, though the fight was obviously taking its toll. Steaming black liquid seeped from deep scratches on the demon's face, legs and torso. The cat's flanks heaved with each breath and dark blood gleamed on black fur in the light of the burning stable.

"Grug!" a voice called, and Grug turned to see Samuel helping a man through the gate at the other end of the stable yard. Grug realized that it must be the captive from the noble's house, though that seemed years before. The thief paused to ease the man down between Triwathon and Haeronor, then hurried up beside Grug, holding a clay pot. "I brought the salt. Is there any way we can pen him in and send him back?"

Grug bit his lip while his mind raced, thinking back through everything Haeronor had ever mentioned about demons and ritual magic. "I...think so, but I don't know for certain. We should be able to hold him in the circle, at least, but we're going to need him to stay in one place long enough to place the circle—unless you've brought enough to go around the entire alleyway?"

Samuel opened the top of the crock and looked in. "Ahh...no. I'd guess we've got enough for maybe a six foot circle...and probably only one shot at that."

Grug grunted sourly, looking back to the fight, where the cat was clearly starting to falter. "I don't think we've got much time, either. What we need is a distraction." Sheathing his sword, Grug took his axe into his right hand, bouncing it slightly in his grip. "Here goes nothing."

Grug stepped into full view of the alley, bones rattling. He glanced back to where Samuel was standing, confusion written plainly on his face. "Go, NOW!" Pulling back his muscled arm, Grug aimed for a spot at the demon's back and threw with all his might. The clattering in his head stopped as the axe buried itself to the haft in the demon's back, just below its neck. The demon squealed in anger and pain, dropping to its knees and twisting its arm in nearly impossible angles in an attempt to grasp the axe handle.

Samuel, already sprinting forward, pulled the lid off of the clay pot and made a swift circle, dribbling salt in his wake. The cat, pushed nearly to its limit, either realized the thief was a friend, or was too exhausted to move; it swayed on its haunches, panting and bleeding from dozens of wounds as the thief made his circuit. If the demon noticed the thief running past it, or had any idea what Samuel was up to, it showed no signs of it; its screeches and struggles continued.

His run completed, Samuel came back to stand next to Grug. “How do we know if it worked?”

“I don't know,” Grug replied. “Maybe we just have to wait until it tries to break out.”

“What about the cat?”

Grug looked over to where the cat now lay on its side, panting and clearly in pain. “I don't think there's much we can do for it right now, either. It's as likely to take our heads off as thank us.”

The two stood in silence but for the crackle of flames and the sounds of breaking timber. Grug was startled to realize that ranks upon ranks of eyes gleamed just outside of the light cast by the burning building. At least a hundred people shared their vigil, but clearly chose not to come any closer to a demon and a cat bigger than a wagon. Grug couldn't really blame them for that.

The demon, still struggling to reach Grug's axe, seemed unaware that his circumstances had changed until a low chanting arose from the stable yard. Haeronor, his face still the colour of old milk curds, had struggled to his feet. His eyes were locked, unwavering, on the unholy beast before them, and they shone with icy determination. The demon froze like a deer in the gaze of a wolf, its face upraised and its nostrils quivering. Suddenly, it darted forward, its face contorted in anger and malice, and its claws out-thrust to rend the puny mage that dared challenge it.

With an impact that cracked cobblestones beneath its feet, the demon crashed into an invisible wall, rising from the salt circle into the night sky. Rebounding into the road, its wings flexing feebly in an attempt to regain its balance, the demon roared in pain and anger. Axe quivering grotesquely with its every movement, the unholy terror regained its feet and staggered to the salt line, its claws frantically scraping at the walls of its invisible prison, searching for any weakness—but the thief had done his work well.

Glowing dimly, the salt rose into the air, forming a dome around the monster. Slowly, but inexorably, the dome began to contract, the grains of salt swirling around the perimeter, and flowing ever inward. Desperate, and clearly afraid, the demon was slowly pushed back into the middle of the circle, its claws still scraping ineffectively at the air around it. As the ring tightened around the monster, the salt grains began to burst, each spattering like a droplet of water on the demon's scaly hide, until he was coated in a crystalline shell. The beast roared once more at the pathetic mortals that had somehow defeated it, but no sound escaped the terrible cocoon. As the shell continued to shrink, a black void appeared in the demon's belly. Slowly, as though pulled through a navel it didn't possess, the demon funneled through the void and vanished.

Grains of salt, solid once more, rained down into the street and were lost in a sudden gust of wind.

Samuel shared a look with Grug. “Is adventuring with you always this exciting?” the thief asked. Grug chuckled. Soon he was roaring with laughter, doubled over and gasping for air. Samuel joined in, his eyes streaming. Even Haeronor, wan as he was, began to laugh softly.

Hobbling past them, the mage approached the cat, whispering soft words in elvish as he stroked its bloody flanks. Grug's laughter trailed off, and he felt his heart swell with love and gratitude toward the brave animal that had risked its life to try and destroy something evil in this world.

The soft golden glow returned almost reluctantly to Haeronor's hand as he continued to pet the cat. By the time the mage stood, swaying drunkenly, a normal-sized, and clearly healthy, barn cat lay at his feet, purring in its sleep.

CHAPTER 9
WHEN THE DICE STOP

Grug slowly awoke to the familiar sounds of raucous laughter. The scent of stale beer and unwashed bodies tickled at his nose, and an ache in his backside suggested he'd been sitting on a hard wooden chair for hours. With a sharp breath in, he came awake in his own body in the comfortable common room of the One-Eyed Jack, across the table from Samuel.

The surprise in Samuel's eyes said that he had just arrived as well. "Gods above!" the thief spat. "Do you ever get used to that?"

Grug grinned. "I'll let you know." A quick sniff of his tankard confirmed it held ale, and Grug took a deep pull from it. He grinned; it was still cold, too.

Samuel looked around. "I take it everything worked out then?"

"You tell me."

Samuel sat back a moment, sorting through his memories. Grug did the same. From what he could recall, Bhalon had been taken to a local healer, where Haeronor helped remove the rest of the arrow and close the wound. Triwathon had recovered, as well, with little more than a memorable headache for his misadventure.

"What happened with the captive?" Samuel asked. "Was he really the king's nephew?"

Grug nodded. "From what I gather, yes. And his uncle was very grateful to get him back."

Samuel grabbed reflexively at his belt pouch. His eyes widened.

Grug laughed. "Don't get too excited. The guild's share is in there, too, though little enough came from loot. Most of it seemed to disappear with the mage—or at least most of it that was worth any coin. There were racks and racks of clothes, though, in case you're looking for a new outfit."

"Clothes?" Samuel asked. "Why would he have kept all the clothes?"

Grug sighed, looking warily at the rest of the inn's patrons for a moment, before leaning in close across the table. "If you could make yourself look like anyone else, what would you need to complete your disguise?"

Samuel paled, and his eyes darted quickly around the room to see if anyone appeared to be listening to their conversation. "He could be anyone, then, couldn't he?"

"I suppose so, but I think...I don't know, but I think we have to be with the rest of the group for him to show up. Almost like he's not a part of this..."

"Storyline?" Samuel suggested.

"That sounds crazy, doesn't it?" the barbarian asked.

"Mildly insane, yes. It fits, though, doesn't it? Especially with the dice."

Grug looked puzzled. "Dice?"

"Of course. No respectable swindler is going to mistake that noise. Those aren't bones, my friend, those are dice rattling together."

Grug realized his mouth was agape and snapped it shut. "If those are dice, then who's rolling them?"

Samuel smiled. "Are you a religious man, Grug? It sounds to me like the gods themselves have taken an interest in you."

Grug could think of nothing to say to that.

"As strange as it sounds, though, I think we may have bigger worries," Samuel said.

"How so?"

"Have you considered why he might want control of the kingdom?"

"Money?" Grug ventured.

"A man with his kind of powers won't hurt for money; at worst, he could impersonate nobles and take money right from their banks," Samuel said. "No, what he wants is power."

"But we already know he wants to impersonate the king. How much more powerful could he be?"

Samuel smiled ironically. "Why stop at one kingdom? Why not the world? Why not the worlds beyond the human ones?" He paused a moment, in thought. "No, I don't think our sorcerer will stop with just one country, any more than he would stop with only one city. Worse, what does a man like that do with that sort of power once it's in his grasp?"

Grug shuddered. "Challenge a god?"

Samuel laughed. "I don't think any man can do that, but there are plenty of other terrible things below that."

The thief pushed back his chair and stood. "I have to check in with the guild and see how much my apprentice has stolen from the coffers in my absence. I'll be damned disappointed with him if it's less than half of what I had stowed—or at least half of what he knows about." Samuel's grin disappeared, and he leaned close. "Watch your back, Grug. I don't pretend to know the gods' plans, but they clearly include you. I don't think they have a quiet future in mind, somehow."

Grug nodded absently in farewell and leaned back in his chair, deep in thought, as the thief threaded his way through the busy common room and into the street.

Dice. Now that Samuel had pointed it out, Grug didn't know how he had ever mistaken the sound for anything else. What it implied, though, was staggering. If it was the gods—and who else could it be—why would they be dicing over the things he did? Why would they be interested in him? It could be the amulet, he reasoned. It was almost certainly the amulet that had allowed him to hear the dice in the first place; perhaps the gods interest had nothing to do with him at all, and it was really the amulet they were concerned about.

Grug mulled that thought around with another swallow of ale. If it was true that the gods were only interested in the amulet, then why had everything else changed? Everything he had heard, the vague, almost fabricated way that he remembered his past, the way he suddenly appeared on adventures without really having experienced the preparations, and then was just as suddenly back in his inn's common room, all felt somehow...familiar. It felt like those things had been true of his life before the amulet, just at the edge of his awareness.

So then what? If the gods, perhaps the High Lord himself, had taken an interest in him, what did that make him? A paladin? Grug chuckled at the thought, nearly choking on a mouthful of ale. Somehow, he didn't believe think he was paladin material, though he wondered if Bhalon had ever felt that way before he was chosen by the High Lord. Grug wished Bhalon was here now. The stolid cleric always seemed to know what to do.

A group of adventurers sat in the corner of the common room, drinking and laughing uproariously. Grug watched them for a moment and thought about joining them. Surely, they'd share a tankard with him—especially if he was paying.

Grug pushed back his chair with a sigh and emptied his tankard. There would be time enough tomorrow for such things; his mind was too heavy, and he was too tired tonight. Dropping a few coppers on the table for the barmaid, Grug made his way to the stairs.

Harsh, orcish consonants caught at Grug's ear as he reached the landing of the upper floor, and he paused on the other side of the thin wall separating the first room from the hall. The inn's patrons were mostly labourers and tradesmen—something that had drawn Grug to it in the first place, as he was rarely made to feel stupid or foolish in their company—and an orcish patron was not terribly unusual. What caught Grug's attention was the volume; try as he might, he could not remember hearing an orc speak softly before—ever. Yell, absolutely; bellow, of course; but speak in a near-whisper? Never.

Grug checked the corridor and quietly snuck closer to the door, careful to keep his feet well away from the door itself, and avoid casting shadows beneath it. The time he had spent drinking alongside orcish laborers paid off; he found that, if he concentrated, he could begin to piece together what was being said: "no go...much danger...steal...worthless...neck trophy." Grug frowned as he puzzled his way through the words, nearly jumping out of his skin as a heavy thud echoed from the room. "Get paid...no matter...steal...neck trophy...kill big man...tonight."

Grug's blood ran cold as the pieces fell into place. He had a pretty clear idea of who exactly the "big man" might be, and what "neck trophy" they were looking to steal. He was more than happy to supply the "danger" for them. The barbarian slipped away from the door with a stealth unexpected in a man his size, and walked quietly up the stairs to his room.

Grug stopped abruptly when he reached his door. Who was to say that the orcs were the only ones plotting against him tonight? Grug listened for the dice, but the gods were leaving him no clues, this time. Quietly, he lowered himself to the floor and peered beneath his door; darkness. Pushing silently up to one knee, he listened at the keyhole; nothing. As quietly as he could, Grug unsheathed his sword, holding it ready while he slipped his key into the lock and turned it. The tumbler boomed like thunder to Grug's ears, almost certainly audible down at the harbour.

Taking a deep breath, Grug threw the door open, launching himself through the doorway in a roll, and springing to his feet, sword in hand, and already committed to a powerful swing. His opponent fell, cleaved nearly in two by his blow, and falling both silently and without blood. Grug stood over him, resignation on his face. He had really liked that cloak, and the innkeeper's invention—a cloak rack, he called it—would never be the same.

When no one came running, it seemed safe to say that his room was empty, so Grug quickly closed the door and began to prepare for the night's invasion. The pieces of the cloak rack he placed in the shadow cast by the moonlight across his pallet. The cloak itself was rolled and bundled, stuffed beneath his blankets to make it look as though he was asleep, and the door was locked again. Then there was nothing for Grug to do but sharpen his axe—and wait.

* * *

It was still hours until dawn, and the sounds of the common room had long since quieted. Grug sat in the shadows of his room, with only a few wisps of moonlight drifting in through the large, curtained window. His axe sat across his knees, its head covered with a cloth. Muffled footsteps sounded outside of the door, and Grug shifted to put his legs under him, ready to spring.

The lock gave way with a soft click and the door swung open enough to admit five black-cloaked figures, blades naked in their hands. Shining swords rose as they moved toward the pallet, standing out from the wall.

With a roar, Grug threw himself forward, the head of his axe cleaving through the front of the closest figure's face. The orc dropped, screaming through a ruined jaw, and Grug reversed his swing, tearing out its throat.

The remaining four men stood in startled shock at the furious barbarian before them, and Grug took full advantage of their hesitation, pressing forward toward them. One man tripped on the remains of the cloak rack, and Grug battered away his sword and buried his axe in the man's chest. Grug let the man fall, with his axe still buried to its eye, drew his sword from its sheath and stood ready, facing the remaining three men. Recovered from their shock, they attacked in unison, though hampered by the pallet, and Grug was dismayed to hear the dice begin to roll in his head. Cursing the gods and their interference, Grug angled to the side to put the third man between him and the other two. With the odds effectively evened, if only for a moment, Grug pressed his advantage and attempted to batter the assassin's sword aside, as he had done with the previous man, and run him through.

The dice stopped.

Grug watched in stunned disbelief as his sword dropped from his hand, bounced on the floor, and gashed his leg. Stumbling backward to gain space, the barbarian reached for his dagger, only to find that the sword had somehow cut through his belt, as well, leaving him weaponless.

The hilt of a sword cracked against Grug's temple, and the room spun sickeningly around him. He felt more than saw two men take his arms, unable to summon any force to oppose them. As he fought to focus his eyes, a sixth figure appeared, seeming to coalesce from the shadows themselves. Grug's stomach lurched as he recognized the sorcerer's face; "Darathan," his mind supplied unhelpfully.

Darathan smiled triumphantly, reached up, and unfastened the chain from Grug's neck. Grug tried to head butt the sorcerer, but found himself unable to move. "I told you I would have the amulet, boy. You should have just given it to me when you had the chance. Perhaps I would have had mercy." He placed a hand on Grug's chest. "Then again, perhaps not."

A surge of power roared into Grug, blackening his skin and hurling him through the window. As he plummeted to what was surely his death, Grug's brain repeated "Grug in trouble" over and over again.

Did you enjoy Dicing with the Gods? Why not join my mailing list at www.nerdincognito.com/Grug-Smash ? You'll get the inside scoop on my new books before they come out, and access to all sorts of great blog content!

Did you know that self-published authors depend on reviews to drive their book's ranking and increase sales? Please take the time to review Grug Smash on Amazon and help me produce more quality content!

A Sneak Peek from Grug Smash Book 2:
Stealing From a Sorcerer

15th Turning, Moon of Magora, 423 D.E.

The barbarian has slept for 3 days. The healer doesn't know if he will ever wake, though he says that the way Grug moves and mumbles in his sleep is a good sign. For my part, I find it hard to credit that his life would end here—it seems a poor ending to an interesting story.

"Put it back, Jamis," the thief said, almost fondly. A young, tousle-haired pickpocket dropped the hilt of Grug's sword with a yelp and scurried from the room.

It's been a task in itself just keeping the barbarian's equipment from growing legs and wandering off—and the two pickpockets that were posted to the inn and saw Grug fall are the worst of them; they act as though everything he held is some sort of holy relic.

"Master Cooper?"

Samuel looked up at the blond, teenage girl on the other side of his desk and smiled. "Cheryl. How are things at the Angry Badger?"

"Good, Sir. Aldrid sends his greetings, and his dues." She put a small, linen purse on the desk.

"Excellent." He looked at the girl for a moment, taking in the thinness of her wrists, and the sharp contrast of collarbones above her small breasts. "How is Aldrid treating you, child?"

Samuel watched the girl's eyes drop to her feet. "Fine, Master Cooper."

"Cheryl." The girl's eyes crept back up to meet his. "If he's treating you well, then why haven't you been eating? You're naught but bones."

The girl coloured, but stayed silent.

Samuel clicked his tongue on his teeth and sighed. "Marcus will accompany you back to the inn and remind Aldrid of his obligations. Has he laid hands on you, as well?"

Cheryl's colour deepened, but she met Samuel's eyes and shook her head. "No, Sir, but the way he looks at me..."

Samuel nodded. "You wouldn't be the first with him. Marcus will deal with that, as well."

"Thank you, Master Cooper."

"Now, have you any news?"

Cheryl pulled a strand of yellow hair to her mouth and chewed the end as she considered the question. "Well, there's still lots of talk about the fire and what happened..." She trailed off for a moment, and her eyes wandered over to Grug's sleeping form, tracing the broad swell of his chest and arms. "You'll know about that already, of course."

Samuel sat, stony-faced. It had been all he could do to keep the stories and rumours in check about Grug and the guild's involvement in the fight with the sorcerer-raised demon. The resulting fire, which destroyed a stable, a farrier's, and an inn before it could be extinguished, didn't help matters.

Sensing Samuel's tension, the girl rushed on. "Some of the border soldiers coming back from tours have been talking about armies growing over the wall."

Samuel arched an eyebrow. "Which countries?"

"To hear them talk, Sir, it's all of them."

Samuel leaned back in his chair. This was the third, separate report he'd had of increases to neighbouring armies; it didn't bode well, especially with the sorcerer unaccounted for and, presumably, the amulet in his hands. It was past time that he reached out to the other guild masters, but he didn't look forward to the instability that would ensue.

Abruptly, Samuel realized that he was frowning at the girl, who was nervously chewing her hair and fidgeting under his gaze. Gently, Samuel reached out and plucked the yellow strand from the girl's mouth, just as she had the first day that he met her, as a newly-orphaned girl of ten, tears clearing paths through the dirt on her face.

"You'll ruin your hair, child."

Cheryl smiled. "I know, I know."

Samuel pulled a silver from the linen purse still on top of his desk and pushed it back across the desk. "For your information. Thank you."

Dimples flashed on Cheryl's cheeks. "Thank you, Master Cooper."

"Marcus!" Samuel called toward the door. A tall, well-muscled man, with old scars snaking crookedly out from the sides of his mouth, poked his head in the room. "Take Cheryl back to The Badger. Remind Aldrid of his obligations when hosting guild foundlings."

The man nodded, his face grim.

"And Marcus? Remind him what we do to men who can't keep their hands to themselves. Gently, but firmly."

Something dark flickered behind Marcus' eyes. He opened the door to let Cheryl through, nodded at Samuel, and closed the door behind them.

It has been difficult keeping the guild out of the guards' scrutiny, as rumours of my involvement in the fight and the fire that followed have spread. Worse, though, has been the scrutiny from within the guild itself. I'm already young to be a master, and many senior members point to the present difficulties as evidence of poor leadership. For my part, I've tried to argue that something far larger looms on the horizon, threatening to swallow us all. Ears that want to hear have listened, and I must hope that it is enough.

Grug tossed restlessly in his slumber, fighting the blanket that caught at his legs. Samuel watched, waiting to see if Grug's eyes would open. After a moment, the barbarian settled again.

Many members also believe that Grug's continued presence is a liability. His fight with the demon, and his fall from the inn's window, have fed public curiousity endlessly, and a reward has been offered for him, though it's said they want only to question him. I am skeptical.

A soft knock sounded at the door.

"Yes?"

Jamis' dark eyes peered through the doorway. "Master Cooper? They're ready for you."

Samuel sighed deeply and stretched his shoulders back at the mere thought of defending himself before the guild elders yet again. "Thank you, Jamis. Tell them I'll be along shortly."

Jamis nodded briefly, closing the door once more.

Perhaps I'm jumping at shadows, but it seems as though the kingdom has changed almost overnight. The guards have always been professional (and stubbornly difficult to bribe), but now they seem aggressive. Even merchants are no longer safe, nor are thieves, or those known to have consorted with thieves in the past. They are taken for questioning...and none of them have yet to return.

I will do what I can to keep the barbarian safe from guards and my own guild, but it seems but a matter of time before one or the other finds their way to him. He had best be awake and on his feet when that happens—I may need someone to help pull a dagger out of my back.

Samuel put down his pen, dusting the final words with sand with an air of old habit. Then he tore the pages from his book, leaving another torn strip in a forest of ragged edges. Collecting the pages together, he turned to the fire burning in the rough stone hearth near the bed. Patiently, and carefully, he fed each page into the flames, watching until he was sure nothing remained by grey ash.

Dusting the last vestiges of sand and ash from his hands, Samuel stood and put his hand gently onto Grug's shoulder. “Sleep well, my friend, but heal quickly. You're needed.”

About the Author

Sean McKenzie is a father of two young boys, a devoted husband, an English M.A. degree holder, and an unabashed nerd. Bitten by the literary bug at a very early age, Sean has written dozens of short stories, plays, and, now, novels, but the Grug Smash series is the first to proceed to publication.

Sean also produces content for his website, www.nerdincognito.com, where he writes blog posts and articles about writing, literature, politics, fatherhood, DIY projects, and other nerdy pursuits.

Made in the USA
San Bernardino, CA
25 September 2016